THE MORBID KITCHEN

THE MORBID KITCHEN

Jennie Melville

Chivers Press • Thorndike Press
Bath, Avon, England   Thorndike, Maine USA

ZE LS BDV2 BC VE PT

This Large Print edition is published by Chivers Press, England, and by Thorndike Press, USA.

Published in 1996 in the U.K. by arrangement with Macmillan London, an imprint of Macmillan General Books.

Published in 1996 in the U.S. by arrangement with St. Martin's Press, Inc.

U.K. Hardcover ISBN 0–7451–4904–9 (Chivers Large Print)
U.K. Softcover   ISBN 0–7451–4916–2 (Camden Large Print)
U.S. Softcover   ISBN 0–7862–0642–X (General Series Edition)

The text of this Large Print edition is unabridged.
Other aspects of the book may vary from the original edition.

Set in 16 pt. New Times Roman.

Printed in Great Britain on acid-free paper.

British Library Cataloguing in Publication Data available

Library of Congress Cataloging-in-Publication Data

Melville, Jennie.
   The morbid kitchen / Jennie Melville.
      p.   cm.
   ISBN 0–7862–0642–X (lg. print : sc)
   1. Large type books.   I. Title.
[PR6063.E44M67   1996]
823′.914—dc20   95–53281

21.95

LIST OF NAMES

Charmian Daniels
Humphrey Kent
Winifred Eagle
Alice (Birdie) Peacock
Emily Bailey
Nancy Bailey
Jim Towers
Superintendent Henry Gervaise Horris
Big Albert
Eddy Bell
Margaret Drue
Madelaine Mason

THE MORBID KITCHEN

THE WAY IT WENT

The house groaned and moved in the wind; even when there was no wind and the rest of Windsor was still, it seemed as though the house had movement in it. Sometimes the neighbours thought that they heard voices and saw lights. But they knew that the family never came back.

The street lamp outside shone into the dead, dark windows which gave back no reflection. Somehow this made the house even more depressing to those who lived near. It was a small road of five houses with large gardens at the back. This house, which had once been a private school, had the largest garden of all, stretching back and back into what had once been fields but was now rough open ground.

The ancient town by the river was changing; a new road was going to be cut through which would touch many lives, but the house was not forgotten. People talked in the town, talked about the house and what happened there. What exactly had happened there? The mystery clung on. There were certain people who spoke of it only in the privacy of their own families. They were all of them people whose lives had been touched by the house.

In its former life, that is, for the house had no life now, and had not had for some ten years. In

1

this time, the town of Windsor had endured great winds, floods and fire, but the house in the quiet road had rotted on. The years of neglect and avoidance had taken their toll so that the windows let in water and the roof had begun to sag. A sad old house.

Dr Yeldon said to his wife, a tall, once beautiful woman whom he held in great respect and some awe: 'I don't like to think of that dread place, my dear. It's not better for being empty. Bad, bad.' She nodded gravely and with dignity; she had once been a dancer and still had great presence. Her husband was not the only one to find her formidable.

Eddy Bell, who was a builder and although still young was, since the early death of his father, now the boss of the family firm, thought about the house sometimes and then would say: 'I see her around the town sometimes, the young one. I wonder what she remembers.' He had his own memories of the house which he preferred not to share, although he alluded to it obliquely to his assistant and mate, Albert. Albert never spoke much to anyone, a lonely soul.

Maisie Nisbett, who had worked in the kitchen with her aunt when it had been a school, was willing to talk about it, although her aunt, now aged, was not. 'Auntie, do you ever go back in your mind to Miss Bailey's School?'

Archie Rose, a nice old man, a widower

2

living with his married daughter, and who had been gardener at the house, walked past the house once a season to see what the bushes he had planted in the front garden were doing (they needed pruning and cutting back, and he speculated sadly on what must be the overgrown state of the back garden). Then he would go home and make jokes about what might have been buried in that garden.

Harry Fraser, who had taught music, and his wife Eleanor, who had taught dancing, also spoke about the house and what had gone on there. If it had actually taken place in the house, because some people, although not the police, thought the killing might have been committed elsewhere, say in a van or a car, and the body brought back. 'A mystery still,' he said. 'I hate to think of it.'

And then there was Madelaine Mason, who had been the matron as well as a teacher and probably knew more than anyone about everyone in the school, but she never gossiped and had left Windsor. What she knew about it, one could only speculate. Young Emily Bailey probably knew her as well as anyone but if asked would have said: 'There is something profoundly odd about this lady that I do not want to speak about now.' She never did want to speak about Maddie. Nor, more than she must, about the woman called Margaret Drue, who had been a teacher at the school at the time of the tragedy, and another player in the

3

game. There was a sense in which Emily spoke as the voice of the house.

Several other people, including the local postman and a young policeman, had come under some suspicion at first and perhaps it had never been totally lifted from them. 'You felt it,' as Harry Fraser said. The postman had died several years ago, still troubled by the finger of suspicion that had pointed at him briefly.

The policeman was still alive and, being a policeman of the new school, was doing some research and getting material together for an article he was going to write for the *Police and Forensic Science Journal* into 'The Place of the Head' in a murder. He had a lot of material already and was shaping the sentences in his head a lot of the time. His wife did not like it and said so: she was a wife of the new school too, and had her own career and her own strong views on life and death, as well, for that matter.

And recently Charmian Daniels, a top-ranking policewoman who lived in the ancient and beautiful town of Windsor, had occasion to think about the house. She had not been personally involved, but she was interested.

But it was the young policeman, knowledgeable about this and that, becoming learned on the history of death and crime, who spoke of the 'Morbid Kitchen'.

CHAPTER ONE

'So this is the house?' Charmian Daniels stared upwards. She was a slender, tall woman who had taught herself to be elegant, to wear her clothes well, and to have her reddish hair well cut. Recently, she had known great happiness and great sorrow. The two seemed to run together in her life.

The house was of four narrow storeys, one in a terrace of five in a small street which ended in a dark passage. The terrace faced the high wall of an old factory. Oddly enough, because the wall was built of good red brick and had weathered well, the effect was not unpleasant. Round the corner there was a large public garden so that there was no sense of being hemmed in. Beyond the other corner was the Maiden Street Police Station. A fine Victorian building and guardian to good behaviour and no crime, you might think. It was threatened with closure now.

The house itself presented a thin face to the world, with two windows on each of its three floors. There was also a basement with one shuttered and barred window. At some time back, a long time by the look of it, the house had been painted white from top to bottom, but the years had turned the white to yellow and streaked it with damp. From the overhang of the roof, as well as from the windows, darker streaks ran like tears. The other houses in the road were well cared for with fresh paint and polished brass on the doors and window boxes full of flowers. They were lived in, cared for; this house was not. 'How long has it been empty?'

'Not as long as it looks.' Emily shook her head. 'But Nancy never really lived in it after...' She hesitated. 'Not after the tragedy. You can understand that?' Charmian nodded assent. She could also understand Emily not using the word murder. 'We couldn't sell the house then, no one fancied to live in it, so Nancy hung on.' Emily's voice was clear and light, a lady's voice. She was a tall girl, in her early twenties, not pretty but with a sort of gawky charm. 'But she was away as much as she could be.'

Which was quite a lot, judging by the state of the house; you could call it neglected.

'After our father died, she took a flat in River Street, a basement flat that flooded in the winter, pretty dreary. I think she knew already that she had cancer ... And being lame didn't help ... she had an accident with her leg when she was young and it was never truly right ... I'd moved out into lodgings before that. Seemed best. I wanted to be on my own.'

A thoroughly unloved house, Charmian thought, taking another look at the shuttered basement window. Emily saw her.

6

'That was where...' she hesitated. 'Where the body was found. It was the old kitchen when the house was built, but it was turned into the playroom.'

'I know.' Charmian had studied a plan of the house, and she had seen police photographs.

'Not that the murder took place in the house. Or so the police thought ... Forensic evidence seemed to say not ... you'd know more about that than I would, although I've tried to learn and understand ... but for Nancy, being accused of it as she was...'

'Suspected.' Charmian made the correction. No one was ever charged or brought to trial about the dead child. She herself had not been living in Windsor at the time, but she had read up about the case, when Emily had asked her to come with her to the house. 'No case was made out against your sister.'

'Half-sister.'

Charmian nodded. The same father, but different mothers. There was a big age-gap between the two sisters. Nancy Bailey a grown woman when Emily was born. Mother dead, father an enigma. Clever and lost, that was how he came out.

'People used to drive here and sit in their cars to stare, or walk and stand outside and try to look in through the windows. Murder House, they called it.'

It was hard to believe that here had once been Miss Bailey's Nursery School, expensive,

7

exclusive and fashionable. Much sought after because of the style of families who sent their children there. It was good to think your child was sitting next to Lady this or the Honorable Harry so and so, and Little Prince that. Fees proportionately high. An old-fashioned dame school, and therefore highly chic.

'I suppose there are outbuildings?'

'Oh yes. Rows of them, we had a lot of ground at the back. Places to exercise and the dance room. We always had a few boarders too. The basement room was the kids' own place, where they kept their own toys and treasures.' That had made the discovery there all the more painful.

Charmian was curious. 'Were you a pupil?'

'Oh no, they sent me round the corner to the local state school. I was at the big comprehensive when it happened. I didn't pay fees, you see, and I took up a place.'

'I tell you what: I don't think I like your family.'

Emily laughed. 'I didn't always like them myself, but they weren't so bad, and I did love them. Love and liking are not the same.'

As I well know, said Charmian to herself, thinking of the lovers she had not liked, and the first early marriage to an older man who had died, and the new husband she liked and hoped that she loved. It certainly felt like love with all its pains and pleasures.

'And money did count. Then too, my school

was good. I learnt how to use a computer there which I don't think Nancy's babies did.'

'But they were only babies.'

Emily shook her head. 'They were never going to learn. Shooting, fishing, riding to hounds, yes. Computing, no.'

Charmian looked down the basement steps. 'How did you and I meet, Emily?'—I've always wondered if you got to know me on purpose. I certainly meant to know you: I was so interested in the murder. The head, ah yes, the head being missing, that was so strange.

'I came to a lecture you gave in St George's Hall on "Women and the Law" and you frightened the pants off me.'

'But you came back to ask questions, and I thought you were a very bright girl.'

'And I tried to join up as a policewoman because I admired you so much, but I wasn't thought to be quite the right material . . . Well, I suppose they knew about Murder House . . .'

'They wouldn't weigh that in,' said Charmian quickly. But she wasn't sure. It might have happened that way.

'So I'm a law student doing it through the Open University and meanwhile earning a part-time living in Frobisher and Roberts, Solicitors, as a kind of general clerk.'

'And you will do well. It's written all over you. Probably take over Frobisher and Roberts. How is Mr Frobisher, by the way?'

'Long since dead. Roberts too. The senior

9

partner is called Ames.'

'Why am I here, Emily?' said Charmian. 'What is it you want from me?'

Emily looked again at the house. 'I'm trying to sell this house. While Nancy was alive, she wouldn't let that happen. By a family trust, it now belongs half to me, half to a cousin who inherited her share from an aunt in Australia. She lives in Scotland and wants to sell.'

'Right.'

'I don't know how much you really know of what went on in this house.'

'I know a certain amount.'

Ten years ago, just as the summer term was drawing to an end at Miss Bailey's School, one child, a girl, had been missed. Charmian had not been in Windsor at the time, but somewhat later she had arrived in the district as a high-ranking police officer. Since then she had been promoted to be head of SRADIC (Southern Register Documentation and Register of Crime) which meant she saw everything and knew everything. She had also secured for herself a small investigating team. She was a powerful woman. She had recently married a man whose career matched her own.

Charmian had made it her business to study the records of the death. The records officer had said as she handed over the files: 'Some of the details are horrible, ma'am.'

Emily echoed the words. 'I wasn't there when it must have happened, I was at school,

10

but when I got back it was horrible. Someone was screaming and my father was shouting, they had just found the body.'

What there was of it, Charmian just stopped herself saying, but she guessed by Emily's face that she had the same thought.

'She was in the basement room, in one of the cupboards.'

'So I have read.'

'They didn't tell me at the time, I was kept away from it, sent to stay with friends and not allowed to see the newspapers. But I used to go down Peascod Street into the big newspaper shop at the bottom and read them there. So I soon got to know all and more. That's how I knew that Nancy was under suspicion, my father too, I suppose, but the papers seemed to concentrate on Nancy.'

It was her school, after all, she was responsible.

'And my father, he was under suspicion at first, but he was in London for most of the day, so that let him out when the time of death was established. He was working on his book. As for Nancy, there was no forensic evidence that linked her to the dead child. She had no motive, either. No one had a motive.'

Those intangible, motiveless cases were always the hardest, Charmian knew. In the end, you usually turned up a motive. But this murder was so far unsolved, although the savagery of the death suggested there was a strong one.

'Of course, once it was grasped that Margaret Drue was missing, she became the chief suspect. She'd worked with Nancy over a year, been trusted, she was such a good teacher, she taught the very little ones. And that made it worse when we found out.'

'It would do.'

'I liked Margaret but once it was learnt that she had a history of mental instability, and something more . . . well, it looked as though it was her.' Emily's voice was sad.

She liked that woman, Charmian could read the emotion; in that unloving household, they must have been friends. And she was young, the nearest in age to the girl. Emily was so young herself then. What a rotten way to have the adult world forced upon you.

'Strange about Margaret Drue,' mused Charmian, her eyes on Emily.

'It was the end of term, all the staff were looking forward to a holiday. She was all packed, with her bags ready, and she wasn't missed at first.'

Charmian nodded. Such things did happen.

'She was never found. It looked as though she just walked out of the house at the end of her teaching that day and no one ever saw her again. The end of term was always full of confusion. A lot of rush and everyone coming and going . . . Most of the children had been collected, the boarders long since and the day

12

pupils taken off in the school bus before it was realized that Alana was missing. She was always one of the last to go.'

'Who else was there in the school? Not just your family and Margaret Drue?'

'Oh no, you're never alone in a school. There was the lady who cooked and her helper, they would have been in the kitchen. There was the music master and his wife, they taught dancing and singing; there had been a little school concert for the end of term, but they had gone home. The gardener was working still and I seem to remember that some repairs were being planned while the school vacation was on and so a workman was there looking things over. But they were never unwatched apparently ... Hard to believe, looking back.'

'Yes, I would have been sceptical.' She was now. 'You remember it all well.'

'Everyone was questioned, over and over again. Anyone who seemed connected or had even been seen near the school that day. Or any day, it seemed sometimes. All the neighbours, the postman, even he was under suspicion for a bit, I think; the road sweeper, and even a young police cadet because he was seen walking up and down the road. Nothing, of course.'

It was all in the records, Charmian thought, even about the road sweeper, long since dead.

'I thought about it a lot over the years, and I talked about it with Nancy till she died. She never stopped talking about it if she could find

13

a listener.'

After the school had closed, Nancy Bailey had taken a clerical job in the Castle library. She was well liked and always had friends, but she had probably not enjoyed the humble position. No longer Miss Bailey of the school, just Nancy at the desk in the window.

'She loved the school, she'd made it. It was hers, I understood.' The touch of sadness again.

Nancy had her school, Father had his book, what did Emily have?

Emily looked up at the blank face of the house. Next door a curtain stirred as if someone was standing there, looking at her looking at the house. An epitome of what life would always be for her: she was an object of interest.

Charmian registered the movement of the curtain for the quick peep at Emily. She ought to move away from Windsor. Go to London. Leave the country. A good lawyer, and she would be a good one, would never be wasted.

'Do you come here often?' she said.

'Oh, you saw the woman looking at me? I thought you might. She's often there. I suppose she's lonely. Yes, I have been coming lately. Business not pleasure.'

'A good idea to sell.'

'There's something I have to explain, perhaps I haven't given the true picture of how things were. Nancy wouldn't sell the house.

14

She did try to live in it. The school was ruined, done for, all the pupils melted away, except for one—her parents didn't seem to mind, but she went, too, in the end, to a school in the country. She's still in Windsor, at the University, Clara Meldrum. I see her around sometimes.'

So do I, thought Charmian, who, once interested, as she must admit she was, in the long past murder, had been at pains to seek her out. Not to talk to her yet, but to see her. She was at all the concerts. Music mad.

'So your sister did cling on?'

'While Father was still alive. He didn't want to leave his study, he liked working in it.'

And the odd murder in the house had not deterred him.

'But something had to be done before Nancy could face it; she had to make the basement room disappear.' Emily looked down at the basement window. 'We did it ourselves, Nancy and my father, and I helped. We boarded the doors up, painted it over, then hung pictures on the wall. That's how it is now. But to sell, we have to undo it. The room has to come back.' She looked at Charmian. 'I wanted you to be with me when that happened.'

There was too much emotion running loose here. Charmian tried to lighten the mood. 'Do I have to take a hammer to it?'

Emily looked down the road where a small van was just turning the corner. 'No, I have a builder coming to do the work. It won't take

15

him long.' She nodded at the van. 'There he is now.'

Charmian looked; she knew the face. Eddy Bell. 'I know him, I've used him myself. It's a good firm.'

'An old Windsor firm,' Emily answered absently. She turned back to the house, walked up the short path and put her key in the door.

It opened at once, Charmian observed. 'That was easy, keys always stick with me.'

The front door swung open letting a puff of stale air blow over them. Not dirty air, just air that had lost its vitality and turned useless.

Eddy walked in behind them, a shortish, sturdy figure. Bright, alert eyes. 'Here I am, ladies, right on time.'

'Five minutes late,' said Emily, not smiling. 'Come in. You know what is needed?'

'You said.' If she wouldn't talk, then Eddy wouldn't either. Besides, he had another interest: Charmian. He admired her and did not mind showing it. 'Nice to see you, ma'am ... m'lady, I should say. Not the happiest time for you, I'm admitting. I've been working at Mrs Cooper's, building a lift to the nursery floor ... Sad affair but the baby has got a good granny.'

'Yes,' Charmian nodded. She had married recently, which was an occasion for more joy than she allowed herself to show, although Eddy seemed to know, but she had lost a loved goddaughter, Kate, who had died in

16

childbirth. The child was in the care of Kate's mother Anny with visiting rights to the father and also to Charmian, who loved the new baby, but Anny was the determined ruler of the cradle. There was a nanny and an assistant and two nurseries and now a nursery lift. Rich baby.

'Not want for anything that baby,' was how Eddy put it.

'No.' Anny's way of showing love, perhaps her only way. She was an old friend to Charmian, they had been students together and the bond between them was strong. Anny was one of the reasons she had come to work in the south of England, but she could not deny that Anny, always rich, and a brilliant artist, had made a difficult wife and mother. You had to stand away from Anny to live with her, which had been hard for her daughter and husband.

'It's the best way for the child, the father being in the same trade as you, ma'am.' Charmian was married to a man with an inherited title, which Eddy knew and wanted to show, but he also enjoyed calling her ma'am because this was what you called the Queen.

She didn't answer. Kate had married a clever young detective, George Rewley, always part of Charmian's team. There were so many thoughts these days that edged back to Kate and her death, and her husband, Inspector Rewley, was one of them. She saw him almost

17

daily and he never mentioned Kate. Everyone has their own ways of mourning, but she feared for the way he had chosen.

Emily gave her a quick look: she too knew about Kate. Break this up. She turned to Eddy: 'Are you ready?'

Eddy bounced forward. 'Ready, ready. Lead me to it.'

The hall was dark, curtains were drawn on the window at the back of the hall. Ahead was a wide staircase, leading upwards, and further down the hall a series of shallow steps to the basement.

Emily took a deep breath, then walked forward. She was pale but determined. This house was going to be sold, the basement room would be opened up, she had to face it.

After six steps downward, the stairs turned left for the dozen steps to the basement. It was dark down here but Emily pressed a switch and the ceiling light came on to reveal a blank wall which faced Charmian and Eddy as they followed Emily down. She nodded towards the wall. 'We worked as fast as we could, my father who didn't want to help, and my sister and me. She did most of it, I just helped her hammer plywood panels into place. Then we slapped on some paint.'

The white paint had turned a streaky yellow. No undercoat had been used so here and there the wood underneath could be seen. Emily had already taken down the pictures, stacking them

18

on the floor. She nodded at Eddy. 'Here you are. Get on with it, please.' She took a deep breath. 'It has to be done.'

'Right, right.' Eddy shouted up the stairs. 'Come on, Albert, let's have you down here.'

The clatter of metal on the stone stairs, together with the scuffle of heavy footsteps, announced the arrival of Albert with spades, buckets and a variety of sharp and probing instruments. Albert was a hefty, broad-shouldered young man with huge red hands; a cheerful smile stayed always on his face, he seemed to have no other expression, as if he knew he was not clever but also knew his own worth: he could do anything with his hands.

Eddy was serious as he checked over his tools. He selected a large chisel and handed a similar one to Albert in whose large hand it looked tiny. Eddy went up to the wall and patted along it. 'Coming away already in places. You didn't do a good job. Just as well, really.'

Emily did not answer, she was staring ahead without a word.

'Are you going to be all right?' Charmian moved closer to her. 'Why don't you go upstairs? I'll stay and watch.'

Eddy was quick. 'I don't need watching, you ought to know that, ma'am.'

'Not criticizing you, Eddy. I'm curious, that's all. I want to be there.'

'I'm staying,' said Emily. She moved back to
19

the stairs, climbed one step as if getting out of the water, and stood to watch.

Charmian took a pace to stand beside her, discreetly studying her face. Too much emotion floating round here. She tried to puncture the bubble. 'How long did you wait before putting this wall up?'

'As soon as the inquest was over, and the child identified for sure ... not that there was any doubt really.'

'Identification did have its difficulties,' said Charmian, who had read the report and knew the state of the child.

Emily looked pale, but she carried on: 'And a verdict of murder was brought in and Margaret named. Then we did it. It seemed the moment.'

'Whose idea was it?'

Emily looked back to that day in the past. 'It just seemed to happen,' she said. 'Perhaps we all thought of it at once. And when you consider, it wasn't such a bad idea.'

'Is it ever a good idea to hide things away?'

'Oh yes. Sometimes you have to. We all do.'

'But when things come out? And they so often do. Like this room ... Here it is again. You put it to sleep for ten years but now you have had to wake it up.'

'We thought we'd come back to live one day, Nancy and I, when we talked over how we felt about things. And the aunt in Australia said she was going to leave us her share. Then it

20

would have been ours and ours alone. Nance made a will leaving me her share and I did the same for her.'

'But your aunt didn't do as she said she would?'

'No, people often don't when money and property is concerned. That's something I've learnt.'

As they talked, Eddy and Albert had been removing the panels, one by one. Eddy turned to Emily. 'Came away easy enough. They'd have fallen down of themselves if left much longer.'

'We didn't mean them to stay up for ever.'

Revealed was a pair of handsome, heavy oak doors, a little dusty and unpolished after their imprisonment. Eddy tried the handle, but the door did not open.

Emily moved forward. 'It's locked; I know where the key is. We left it inside.' Emily ran her hand along the ledge above the doors. She withdrew her hand. 'Here it is.' She put the key in the lock and turned it. 'We oiled the lock before we shut it all in.'

What a scene it must have been, Charmian thought, a mixture of coolness and panic. Which of the actors provided which emotion?

Eddy tried to go in but Emily pulled him back. 'No, this is for me.'

She threw open the doors, then pressed the switch on the wall so that the centre light came on. 'Still works, I wondered if it would.' A

21

breath of stale, dead air, faintly scented with something or other, so that Charmian sniffed, rose up towards them.

They crowded round the door. The room was empty except for a line of small chairs by the boarded up window. A row of tall cupboards ran along one wall. An old-fashioned cooker with an open grate beside it, rusty now but once blackened and shiny. A thin layer of dust lay over everything, but it was undisturbed. No rodent feet marks or droppings disturbed it.

'The old stove was left,' said Emily. 'In the winter it was so cosy.'

As they looked, one of the doors, disturbed perhaps by the banging, swung open a little way. Something moved behind. A foot-shaped object appeared. Charmian went over and dragged the cupboard door wide apart. A figure was sitting there, legs apart and extended. From between her legs, something round and with hair, rolled towards them.

Charmian turned towards Emily. 'I don't think Margaret left you after all.'

CHAPTER TWO

'So what happened?' asked Dolly Barstow. 'What did Em do?' Dolly had a remote friendship with Emily, the two met occasionally at the pool where Dolly swam. She couldn't count herself as a close friend, but she was prepared to be a supporter. And a close observer. She was very interested.

She was talking to Charmian in the latter's office in one of the older buildings in the town and in which Charmian had created, on purpose, a scholarly book-lined air. It was a sign that she meant to be taken seriously.

It was over an uneasy, troubled week later. Charmian had come to her office from the house in Maid of Honour Row where she and Humphrey still lived while they debated which of the four houses they owned between them they would live in. Humphrey had a handsome town house in Windsor as well as a family home in Berkshire; Charmian had a qualified right to a small village house as well as the house in Maid of Honour Row. It was proving difficult to decide. Meanwhile Muff the cat and Benjy the dog had voted with their feet to stay where they were. The dog was attached to Charmian's neighbours, Birdie Peacock and her friend Winifred Eagle, two charming white witches who kept a benevolent eye on Charmian.

Charmian considered. 'Emily went very white, but didn't faint. It was big Albert that went down.'

'Must have made a racket.'

'Like a building coming down.'

Albert had lain prone on the floor like a
23

great oak tree or whole church tower collapsed, but none of those remaining upright had moved to help him, all three had their eyes on the scene before them. The crouching, bent dusty figure with the head, small and childish, on the floor between its knees, like an anatomical drawing, a sketch by a wandering artist of the ruins of medieval Rome, with art and history all combined.

'It was a shock.'

'I bet. But she's tough, Em, I've always thought so.'

'I didn't feel too good myself,' Charmian admitted. 'I've got soft since the old days. I don't often seen an unburied corpse at SRADIC.'

'We've buried a few.' As Sergeant Dolly Barstow she had taken study leave to add to her academic qualifications (a course which made Charmian, who long since left academia behind, slightly uneasy. Who was treading on whose footsteps? But she admired, liked and trusted Dolly, while feeling the force of her ambitions). Dolly had now returned to work with Charmian in SRADIC at the rank of Inspector. 'So what happened now you had turned up the body of the long lost?' She paused and added softly, because it really was a sickening thought, 'Together with the missing head.'

Charmian took a sip of her office coffee, which was good, being made on her own machine with her special mocha blend; she had got fussier about what she drank, the older she got. In her green days she had happily swallowed mugs of lukewarm, standard issue powdered coffee. No longer, it was another sign from her that you took her seriously, or else.

'We couldn't take it for granted that we had the body of Margaret Drue and the head of Alana Heston, although it certainly seemed likely.' Charmian shrugged. 'You know how it goes. I made a few telephone calls and the usual chorus arrived.'

In dribs and drabs.

A patrol car first, with two uniformed officers, one a woman, eyes filled with interest at what had turned up on a dull day, but being carefully polite to Charmian. They all knew her, even when she did not know them.

Then a detective sergeant with a woman detective, and soon after this two scene of the crime officers appeared. Then the police surgeon.

The photographers arrived next, two of them, plus the usual equipment.

The machine was rolling, and downstairs in the basement it was beginning to get crowded. Charmian found that she knew many of the faces and most of the names.

'What happened to big Albert?' He had once repaired her roof, badly as it turned out and it still leaked, but Dolly remembered him.

'He was revived by Eddy, or revived himself, I wasn't noticing. He's still breathing, so don't worry. I think they went to sit in their van to await being questioned. Emily and I sat on the stairs to the basement to watch.'

The police team would have preferred it if Charmian had left but were not in a position to pull rank.

'Some more coffee? They wanted me out,' Charmian confessed honestly, 'for which I don't blame them, but they couldn't see their way to it ... I had been there when the body and head appeared. Like magic it was, in a terrible kind of way, and I was a witness.'

She sat back in her chair, remembering the scene. The police surgeon had not occupied himself long, before standing up. 'Well, she's dead all right. You don't really need me to tell you that. And has been, poor lady, for some years. Yes, a female, and underneath the clothes she is more or less a mummy. I can't say how she was killed but it looks as if she was strangled. The post-mortem and the pathologist will give you all that.'

Dr Fullyer, yes that was his name, picked up his bag; his job was done, he had declared the corpse dead.

'About the head, well, nothing much to say there, just a skull,' he frowned, 'although to be fair, there is more flesh and skin than one might expect. Judging by the bones, a child and by the hair, a girl. But that's guessing.'

Dolly sipped her coffee. She appreciated good stuff. 'Who was there?'

Charmian ticked them off on her fingers. 'Jimmy Towers.' An inspector now, these last two years, a decent if not clever fellow, and said to be bookish by his mates, whatever that meant. He had some special interest, what was it now? 'His sergeant with him, I know his face, I think he's called Flail.'

'Will Flail, I know him. He's clever enough but a bit of a bully if you let him.'

'I'm sure you don't.'

'He's learning,' said Dolly grimly. Their paths had crossed in the days before she had joined Charmian at SRADIC. 'Who else was there?'

Charmian looked down at her hands. 'The photographers were the pair nicknamed Bill and Ben. I don't think I know any other name. The scene of the crime people, I don't remember the names, not important. The pathologist was Lloyd Jordan.'

Dolly spoke with conviction: 'He's good.'

'I could see as a team they would have liked to clean me up with the suction hose that the forensics were going round with sucking up everything on the floor they could lift.'

'But you stayed, beady-eyed.'

'I stayed anyway, and so did Emily, although she looked very green . . . and then H. G. Horris turned up.' Superintendent Henry Gervaise Horris, newly transferred to the

27

district from beyond the darkest reaches of the M40, and always known as HG. But no country bumpkin, he.

Charmian looked back on the scene. A bright top light had been rigged up so the workers could see what they were doing in the darkish basement room. It was making the air hot, and smells of the living and the dead moved on the air. Charmian knew from experience that a mobile incident van was already parked outside, and that the neighbours and a few from the press were outside too. At the moment, early on, it would be the local press and stringers there first, but soon the men from London would be down. It was going to be that sort of case. She had already answered a few preliminary questions, as had Emily, but more would follow for them both. Very soon, if she read the signs right, she and Emily would be offered tea and a ride home. Or in her case, no ride home; without doubt they had already checked the number of the smart red Rover car parked outside and knew it was hers. Indeed, the more worldly among them would have taken the trouble to learn the make and number of her car long since on the grounds that it was as well to know where she was.

Emily had sat next to her on the stairs, close but separate, her body rigid. Charmian had put an arm around her, but had quietly withdrawn it when she felt the unyielding muscles which

28

did not want sympathy.

'It's all right, Emily, we can go away if you like. I'll come with you. Come on, let's go. This is too much for you to bear.'

'No.' Emily stared straight in front of her. 'I'm staying.'

'There's no need, my dear.'

No answer. But Charmian heard a mutter. 'Head man. We need a head man.'

Extraordinary thing to say.

'Yes, that's Em,' said Dolly, as she took this in. 'I've heard her like that; she goes over the top. She ought to talk to Jim Towers, he's interested in heads and murder.'

'But by then,' went on Charmian, 'forensics had come across the big surprise.' She shook her head. 'And then I had to be there.'

'Ah yes, the surprise,' said Dolly. 'Surprised me. What a thing! I was fascinated.'

'Of course you were. Everyone was. The investigating team were. Probably out now checking on my movements on the day she died.'

'Oh yes, where were you?'

'Heaven knows, all those years ago.'

'No alibi then,' said Dolly gleefully. 'You were probably in Windsor being interviewed for that job. Or looking for somewhere to live.'

'Or just visiting my friend, Anny Cooper, who lives in Windsor, as she did then, and whom I have known for many years. Don't forget any of that.'

Hidden in the clothing of Margaret, if that was her name, the police had found a newspaper cutting.

It showed a photograph of Charmian and gave an account of the new appointment she was about to take up, which was not the present one at SRADIC but the more orthodox police role which she had occupied before.

Scrawled on the edge of the newspaper were the words: HELP ME. SAVE ME.

Shortly after this discovery, perhaps deciding that they needed to be on their own, H. G. Horris and Jim Towers had conferred quietly and suggested that Charmian could go home.

'Only if you wish, ma'am,' H. G. had said. 'Delighted to have you stay if you so wish.' He had found his slightly stiff, old world manners a useful tool on many occasions.

She had looked at Emily, who was still not making much of a response but was now clutching a mug of tea which Detective Amaryllis Barton, a kind girl, had handed to her. Horris was drinking his mugful, though.

Charmian had nodded towards Emily. 'I don't want to leave her behind.'

HG had let a doubtful look pass over his face, he wasn't going to let Charmian call the tune. Not any tune. 'It is her house. I might have some more questions, you know how it goes, ma'am, one can't always say in advance.'

Flannel, Charmian summed up. 'She's told you all she knows. Just as I have about the newspaper cutting.'

'Now that is strange.' HG's eyes were bland and yet sharp at the same time. 'Just what you feel ought to be important and yet when we do find out, if we ever do, it may mean nothing much at all.' He shook his head. 'You don't remember the dead woman at all?'

'You don't know for sure who she is yet.'

'It's a pretty good guess though. No, it's Margaret Drue alright. The pathologist will confirm it, you'll see. The clothes look right, and that's where I'd like to have another go at Miss Bailey here. She may remember more if she gets a look at the skirt the woman was wearing. You can see the colours.'

Emily had been listening after all. 'I saw the skirt when we opened the door. It's yellow with a stripe. I don't remember it clearly but I remember a striped skirt, but it's Margaret, I know . . .' She didn't look at either of them. 'And the head, I can tell you whose head it is. I mean, we know, don't we, who lost a head. Alana, Alana. What game are you playing, pretending you don't know?'

HG reverted to the bland approach. 'I think you should get home, miss, we can talk tomorrow. It's early days yet. I'll see you get a lift home.'

'I'll take her home,' Charmian said.

'Good of you, ma'am, thank you.' He tilted

31

his voice from the bland to the gentle rustic. 'Just one last thing. What made you decide to open up the downstairs room today?'

'I have to sell the house. The house agent said it had to be opened before he could put it on the market.'

'And why today, miss?'

'No special reason, the first chance I had, that's all.'

'I see. And you, ma'am?' He turned to Charmian. 'What about you being here? Any special reason?'

'I was asked.'

He didn't have to mention the newspaper cutting with its cry for help. His posture, the swivel of his eyes to the cupboard in the room behind him, told it for him, and he shook his head. 'A coincidence, then, just a coincidence. They happen a lot more than we like to think.'

Coincidence. Charmian raised an eyebrow. I'll think about that one. What is a coincidence? It is arbitrary and unexpected. Does a coincidence mean anything? Or is it just that man is a superstitious animal always looking for the voice from the skies to give an answer? As it happens, I think I detected another coincidence in my quiet look at the corpse, and you must have done so also. And I wonder if you are calling it coincidence.

'We won't bother you, ma'am,' said HG smoothly. 'I'll ask Amaryllis, pretty name isn't it, to take Emily home.' He nodded towards

32

the detective. 'I'll get her to run Emily home.' He lowered his voice, although Emily gave no sign of listening, but kept her eyes fixed on the basement room where the police were working. 'She might talk more freely on the way home to a stranger, and there's a lot there to say, I think.'

You don't look like someone who believes in fairy tales, in spite of your country style, and I'm not sure if you are credible in that role either, because there is a touch of the city in your voice, but you don't expect her to say much to Amaryllis.

You just don't want her to talk to me.

Fair enough.

As she went out to her car, she saw the morose faces of Eddy and Albert peering from their cab window. No home for them yet.

*　　　*　　　*

'As it turned out,' she said to Dolly Barstow, 'I did drive Emily home. I had no sooner got in my car than I was called back. Emily wouldn't leave the house and HG thought I might be the one to persuade her.'

'Did you?'

'In the end. I just took her arm, and told her she was leaving ... She could have walked, she doesn't live far away from the old house. She lives in a grotty bedsit in Habsburg Street.'

'Been there. Did you go in?'

33

'Wasn't asked.'

'It's a tip. She's an unhappy girl.'

Dolly, meticulous herself, found it easy to equate disorder with unhappiness. Charmian, not so tidy, could see the fallacy here. 'She might just be lazy.'

Charmian got up to refill her cup. 'I'm almost surprised that Horris let her go. You could see the questions floating round his head: was the body there when the family covered-in the room? Was the head there too at the same time? Did they put them there?'

'He's bound to start from the idea that they did. And to go from there to conclude that the family did the killings.'

Charmian stared at her coffee cup. 'The elder ones, anyway. Emily was at school.'

'They were suspected at the time of killing the child, but no proof turned up and then when Margaret was missing, that let them off the hook. I was very junior at the time, but I remember the case. It was looked on as a police failure.' She was thoughtful. 'The word was that the team investigating the murder never felt the Bailey father and daughter were in the clear. Chief Inspector Seldon was in charge, I don't know if you ever knew him?'

Charmian shook her head. 'He'd retired before I came on the scene. I've seen his photograph, though, in a group, he was getting a medal or handing one out, he looked a tough.'

34

'He was. I didn't know him well, obviously, but the legend was that he could drink anyone under the table, and that was saying something for then. Things have changed a bit. I was very junior and he was one of what we used to call the old school, and women in his view were there to make tea and see to the children. The fact that I had a degree would have alarmed him even more if he had ever noticed me, I don't think he did. But he had the reputation of being shrewd and thorough. The tale has it that he was never happy about the case; he knew they had never got to the bottom of it. He had to accept that Margaret Drue had killed the child, the coroner's verdict named her, so it was the official line, but I don't know that he ever believed it himself. And of course, they never traced her.'

'She's turned up now,' said Charmian with feeling, 'and with my name in her pocket.'

'I heard it was tucked in her knickers.'

'Her brassiere, in fact.'

'Coincidence, HG called it.'

'Well, it was.'

'I hope so. I swear that Emily did not know it was there, and did not expect to find the body and the head. I saw her face. Let's call it an oddity that I was there and the paper was found.'

'But? There is a but, isn't there?'

'There was another oddity in that room, and one I am sure that Superintendent Horris

35

observed for himself: I saw the neck of the dead woman and I think an attempt had been made to cut off her head.'

Dolly looked at her gravely. 'Just shows the murders were done by the same person.'

'Yes, sure. With a bit of an obsession with heads. The cutting off thereof. And Emily said that we needed a head man, and now you tell me that there was a "head man" present: Inspector Jim Towers. It's too many coincidences for me.'

'I won't hear a word against Jim Towers,' said Dolly.

'Not saying one.'

'He's one of the best young inspectors we've got.'

Charmian grinned at her. 'Like him, do you? Good.'

'He's married.'

'And I suppose you like his wife too?'

Dolly paused. 'She's a bitch.'

'That's a harsh judgement.' And not like Dolly.

'She tells lies.'

'About you?'

'It has been known.'

'Ah.' Dolly had a gift for falling for the wrong men. A married colleague with a bitch of a wife fitting into this category. There was strong emotion here, she was being protective of Jim Towers.

Charmian conceded. 'Let's drop the word

36

coincidence: let's call it a synchronicity of events.'

Dolly looked at her warily. 'And that means?'

'Come on, you're an educated lady. It means a linkage of events.'

'All right, I accept that, events are linked.'

Charmian looked at Dolly and drew her own conclusions. She did not approve of affairs between colleagues but it happened and she was in no position to be censorious, having been down that road herself, but sex always softened Dolly's acuteness and it had done so now.

'I wish I knew how my linkage came in. I didn't get more than a glance at the newspaper cutting (it looked torn rather than cut, by the way), nor the date nor the edition, before the forensic man whisked it away.'

'It was one of the local newspapers.'

'How do you know that? Ah, I know you, your young man leaked it to you.'

A slight pinkiness appeared on Dolly's throat and travelled up to the face. It would have been a blush on anyone less composed, and she admitted nothing. 'Well, it has to be a local newspaper, probably the *Herald*, and he isn't my young man.' She would like to have said: And how's your marriage? I understand that you and Humphrey live more or less split lives. But I expect you would say that was due to your work patterns.

37

'Oh come on, Dolly. You're more than just interested. It's got closer than that. But you're right ... it's none of my business, I won't talk about it.'

'While we're not talking about me, I'll tell you about Rewley.'

Charmian kept in close touch with Rewley both personally and professionally; she was surprised. 'Something I don't know? What is it?'

'He's had a flaming row with Anny Cooper.'

'Everyone always does have a flaming row with Anny.'

Charmian loved her friend Anny, whom she knew George Rewley found a difficult mother-in-law, a tricky relationship in itself so everyone said. She had never had a mother-in-law herself, although she had once been one. Only for a very short time before the relationship had changed into one more dangerous when she had fallen in love with her married stepson. Long past now and better forgotten, except you never did forget. That was the great truth of all time.

'And he's planning to ask for leave, take the child away and bring it up himself.'

'That might not be a bad idea.' It would help his grief for Kate. Mad ideas, which on the surface you could call this one, were often the best. 'But what about the nannies and nurseries?'

'He can't afford those, obviously. He's going

38

to do it all himself.'

'It takes more than one year to bring up a child.'

'Well, he knows that, of course, but you can't think ahead more than that, Charmian. Or I guess he can't. Not at the moment.'

The child was six months old and Rewley was probably only now coming to face the true pain of Kate's death.

Charmian thought about it. 'He's working well, he hasn't let his standards drop.' Dolly Barstow and George Rewley were important workers in SRADIC. 'I know I've kept him on routine work.'

'He knows it too.'

SRADIC, under Charmian's rule, was a feared institution. Ostensibly, the unit oversaw and checked all records, of persons and cases, but Charmian had a watching brief: she could call any record, any person in. To hear that SRADIC had either been called in or was interested struck terror in the bravest investigating team.

She was involved in this new case, whether she liked it or no. 'I might need his help,' she said. 'Work might be best of all for him. And no . . .' she held up a hand . . . 'I know what you are going to say: that looking after a baby is work too. I think he may have to do both. And it might be better for both of them, Rewley needs intellectual satisfaction.'

Dolly was opening her mouth to protest that

39

such an unsubtle comment would never have been made by her, not for nothing had she listened to some of her married friends complaining of the hard slog and low stimulus level of life with babies, when the telephone rang.

It was Jim Towers. And somehow Dolly picked up the tones of his voice. Charmian caught her eye. My God, she really loves this man. And I don't want her to. In my heart I have been saving her up for Rewley. Rewley after Kate.

She remembered some words of Humphrey's after one of her outbursts: life does get out of hand sometimes.

Life had got out of hand again.

He had a pleasant voice, quiet and gentle. 'I thought you would be pleased to know we have found where the newspaper cutting came from: the *Windsor and Datchet Warden*. I've got a photocopy of the whole page, would you like it faxed to you?'

Charmian thought she would like to see him with Dolly, it would help her to understand them. Did he care for Dolly? She wanted to know. 'Where are you?'

'In the office, ma'am.' The office was in the HQ and just across the way from her own office.

'What about coming round?'

Jim Towers hesitated. The body in the cupboard, the head of the child, two cases in

40

one, had caused furious activity in the CID, they were under pressure to produce a result quickly now for the media (how they hated that word, he'd called them the newspapers and the TV and the wireless for as long as he could), but you did not easily turn down a request from the head of SRADIC.

'On my way.'

Dolly had been listening. 'You did that on purpose.'

'No, it's business.'

Jim Towers had wished to come, the newspaper cutting was his way of getting a meeting. He must have something to say, make some point.

The two women sat in companiable silence. Charmian had created an atmosphere of peace in her office on purpose, it was how she wanted to feel when she worked: at one with her pictures and the books on the wall, alert, in this world, but calm. Her neat, portable word-processor had the lid down, while the printer and her fax rested behind closed doors to her right.

He knocked but came in before she answered, though he stood waiting for her to speak. Charmian stood up. 'Come in, sit down. Have some coffee?' She looked at Dolly. 'Pour him a cup, will you?' She held out her hand. 'You've got the paper? Can I have it?'

She bent over it while Dolly attended to the coffee and handed over a cup. Black, no sugar.

41

They avoided touching each other and made no eye contact. So it was serious for both of them, then. She held this thought in her mind while she studied the photocopy, freshly done a few minutes ago judging by its pristine feel.

Yes, there she was, a younger woman by some ten years but not so much changed. Better hair-cut and that figure in the background was surely Anny Cooper outside her own front door. Yes, she had stayed with Anny when she came up to give a talk and that was where the photograph had been taken. She remembered it now.

'I don't suppose it means much to you, ma'am, but do you see the date?'

'August the first? And the child Alana was found dead in July? Is that what you are saying? That Margaret Drue who was missed from before that day was still alive and well afterwards?'

'If she wrote that cry for help,' said Dolly.

Charmian looked at Jim Towers. 'What's the opinion?'

'We think she did. It's a starting point. If she didn't, who did and why? It's too many questions. Forensics may come up with something positive, linking the body and the newspaper cutting. Sometimes it happens.'

'Not always,' said Dolly.

Towers turned to Charmian. 'Could she had known you, or met you?'

Ah, so that's the question you came to ask?

Or perhaps it was the one HG wanted to ask and put you up to it.

'As far as I know we had no contact.' Then, because this sounded bleaker than she wanted it to be, she said: 'But she could have seen me or heard me, I did a few broadcasts and TV interviews about that time. She could have known my name.'

'And, of course, you were not in Windsor at the time.'

Now they were getting down to it.

'I used to stay with my friend, Anny Cooper. I never stayed long, the odd weekend, but I was here quite often ... But as far as I know not at the time the child was killed or immediately afterwards. I had some leave then, and I went away. I had been in Windsor when I was offered my appointment here, and that was the reason for the photograph.'

Jim Towers finished his coffee and put down the cup; he placed it neatly so that the polish of the table at his elbow was not marred.

'I was there,' he said, awkwardly, as if he was shifting a burden from his shoulders and shifting it on to hers.

Dolly make a slight protective movement with her hand.

'I was still in the uniformed branch then, but I had ambitions...' He smiled, revealing the taking young man he must have been. Was still, when less tense. 'I knew I'd make CID, it was coming, but I hadn't got there yet. I'd just

43

been married too.' He shook his head. 'I think it was hard on her.'

'It's never easy.' She was careful not to look at Dolly, wondering what was coming. 'We've all been there.' The platitudes were rising easily to her lips, which was not a good sign.

'Not me,' said Dolly, 'careful not to marry.'

This was true, Charmian acknowledged, but there had been enough love affairs to keep her mind occupied. From the deliberately blank look on Jim Towers' face, she guessed that he had heard this remark before and had made his own riposte. Both parties had set out their stalls and knew what was on offer and what was not. It looked as though he would not, or could not, leave his wife.

'There is a reason for the way I'm talking. I said I was there all those years ago, I didn't tell you that I was the first police officer there when the child's body was found. I was about twenty yards down the street when I heard screams, the front door was flung open and a woman ... later I knew it was Nancy Bailey ... came running out. She had opened a cupboard in a downstairs room and seen...' he stopped. 'Well, I don't know what she had seen, because she slammed the door shut and ran away, but she had seen enough to know it was Alana's body. I opened the door wide: I was the first to see that the child had no head.'

He paused again. 'I was sickened, frightened, and yet ... interested ... I had very

44

little more contact with the case then, I was still in uniform, but I never forgot it. Why was the head cut off? What was so important about the head? I used to think about it, and I came to realize that for some killers the head was very important.'

'Yes, I grant that.' Charmian was watching his face, which was full of thought.

'Some murderers seem particularly sensitive about it. Very conscious of the actual heads of their victims. Nielsen, for instance, cut off the heads of some of the men he killed and kept them in his refrigerator. Maria Madsen buried the heads in a circle round her little wooden house in the Hudson Valley. And each head had a penny on each eye. There is some suggestion that Christie tried and failed to cut the head from one of his victims. In one case, he may have covered the eyes. The Stavanger murderer cut the heads off his victims and gouged out the eyes. He cut the tongues too. PC Gutteridge had his eyes damaged. That gives us a clue, I think. Heads can talk and eyes have seen.

'They are a symbol: think of the heads of those publicly executed in England prior to Victorian reforms. (I don't mean the executions by the axe in the Tower of London, they were political) but the ordinary display of the heads of the dead at Tyburn. It mattered to have the head for public display. As with the use of the guillotine in the French Terror: there

45

were other ways of execution, but cutting off the head said something very powerful.'

'It certainly did,' said Dolly, who seemed in no mood to be agreeable to her lover.

Interestingly, he ignored her. 'In murder, as opposed to judicial execution, I think the killer had superstitious feelings about the head which might shout his name. Whether he or she admitted to this feeling, I am sure it is what lies behind it. The head is dead but can speak.'

'Didn't they rot?' Dolly again.

This time she got an answer. 'In England before those Victorian reforms took hold, the executioners used to boil up the heads first. They boiled them in a stove in what they called the "Morbid Kitchen".'

Dolly was silenced.

'You know your subject,' said Charmian with some respect.

'Yes. And that is why Superintendent Horris has asked me to concentrate on the head. Why it was cut off. Where it has been, and why it was placed with the woman's body where it was found.'

'Difficult questions.'

'Yes. Were both child and woman killed by the same person and the head put in with her body for reasons we don't know? Or did Margaret Drue in fact kill the child and was killed in her turn in an act of vengeance, the head being put in with her to display her guilt? Or did Margaret kill herself, and take the head

46

to her death with her?'

'Is it possible she killed herself?'

'Not likely, I am just throwing up ideas. From the look of her, no, but the pathologists haven't given a definite opinion yet.'

Charmian said, very slowly and carefully: 'I thought I saw signs that an attempt had been made to cut off her head.'

'The Chief would like your help. He knows you are interested. He sent me to ask.'

Charmian looked down at her hands. Fear the Greeks when they come bearing gifts was good advice when dealing with H. G. Horris. What was he after? Help possibly, observation at close hand by Jim Towers, very likely. Anything else?

And what's your motive, Jim? She caught Dolly's intent gaze.

'I've got a lot on hand,' she said cautiously.

'I realize that.'

'I may not be able to do too much myself.' Which was a lie, she was passionately interested, and would certainly be in there. 'But we're a team, I can't give much time, but there's Dolly now she's back from her legal studies, and George Rewley, and I have a couple of young assistants. Nick Elliot and Jane Gibson.'

'I know the names, know Rewley of course. I'm sorry about his wife.'

'Have you got any children?'

He smiled, a tender smile. 'A boy and a girl.'

47

Then he said, as if somehow the two statements were linked, 'I want you to come with me to see Emily Bailey.'

In the outer office she could hear the voices of Amos and Jane, laughter, cheerful sounds, no tensions with them. Then a door banged and silence. She knew where they had gone: they were checking fraud in a chain of bookmakers.

'When do you want to do this?'

'Now.'

'I'll come.'

Dolly stood up too.

'I'll leave you in charge, Dolly. You stay here. Mind the shop.'

Dolly opened her mouth to protest, but shut it again. There were times you could argue with Charmian and times you could not. This was one such.

'Meet me for lunch at the Fisherman's Bar in Datchet and we'll have a sandwich.'

Dolly, who had fully intended to have a sandwich and coffee with Jim Towers, nodded bleakly.

Charmian walked to the door, leading the way. Not my business to break them up, but I wouldn't mind doing it, was her thought.

'Love to Emily,' called Dolly after her.

*   *   *

Emily's drab little room reminded Charmian

48

of her own days in her first job after graduating. She had not gone straight into the police but had taken a job as a secretary. She had not distinguished herself, not helped her employer, a rising young MP, very much but she had taken away from the months they were together a healthy scepticism about public life, and typing skills which stood her in good stead. The MP had paid very little so she could afford only the most modest living space.

Emily let them in. Her reaction to the detective was weary and unfriendly. 'Thought you'd be back.' She made no apology for the disorder of the room where dirty cups rested on a pile of books which in turn sat upon a heap of clothes. A neglected pot plant in need of watering suggested that the owner of the room had once made an attempt at something better. 'I ought to be at a lecture.'

'Hello there.' She managed to smile at Charmian. 'It's good to see you. Thank you for coming. I appreciate it.'

The girl looked as though she had not slept or even combed her hair since last seen. Charmian thought but did not say: I was brought. Don't thank me.

She was still amazed at the way she had fallen in so easily with Towers: he had force, that man. All of which was now about to be directed at Emily.

'Can't you work?' Work had often been her support in time of misery. As well as drink, cigarettes and sex, but better not dwell on times past.

'No.' Emily shook her head. 'Mind won't function.'

Try the other expedient. 'Go out with the boyfriend.'

Emily managed a smile. 'Can't. Quarrelled.'

'Now's the time to make up.' A good reconciliation did a lot for morale. She ignored Towers' impatient shuffle, but a look on Emily's face warned her to keep off the subject of boyfriends. Leave it.

She turned towards Jim Towers. 'It's your party.'

'Would you like some coffee?' Emily made the offer but showed no signs of being ready to do anything about it; she was slumped on her bed which doubled as a divan with the pillows heaped at one end. Charmian guessed the bed was unmade underneath.

'No, thank you.'

'Just as well, not sure if I've got any.'

Emily, Emily, this is not a man to irritate.

'I'm concerned with the head. The head worries me.' There was an echo in his voice of the young man who had first found the headless body of the child Alana. But he looked every one of his thirty-odd years and also like a man who had quarrelled with his wife at breakfast and was not in love with life. 'The head?'

'I'm not overjoyed with it,' said Emily. She

50

drew her legs up on to the bed to crouch like a little cat. 'Come on, get on with it.'

Towers took her through her invitation to Charmian to go with her (this seemed to interest him, as in retrospect it did Charmian herself), the call at the house, then the finding of the body and the sight of the head.

'You know all this,' Emily was showing irritation. 'I've told you.'

Towers bent his head over his notes, which he appeared to be reading but Charmian suspected he was not. Well, she'd employed that trick herself. Unsettling your witness, it was called.

'The old stove in the room, was it ever used?'

Emily frowned. 'It was lit sometimes in winter.'

Towers nodded. 'The oven attached to it, was that ever used?'

'Not as far as I know. It was a Victorian affair, I doubt if it could be used.'

Towers nodded again. 'I have to tell you ... the head had been immersed in water,' he said in a low voice. 'And the water heated.'

Emily stared at him. At last she understood. 'Boiled, is that what you are saying? Cooked?' She began to shake. 'I can't believe it.'

'I must also say that there are traces of human body fat on the sides of the cooker.'

Emily went white. 'Then they must date a very long way back, to the days when the room was a kitchen.' She shook her head as if

51

dispersing the image of a cooking head. 'You know yourself, you must know from the police records, that the house was swarming with police when Alana's body was found. They would have checked everything.'

'Perhaps not the stove, no need then.'

'They would have looked inside.' She swallowed as if there was a lump in her throat. 'And then later the room was boarded up. You know that.'

'Yes, that's what's so interesting,' said Jim Towers, the head man. His eyes were bright and intense.

'I can't help you. I have no answers.'

'No, that's our job.' He didn't look at Charmian, but she got the impression he expected some input.

I'm not a computer, was her reaction, you can't just feed information my way and expect me to answer. 'Someone got into this room,' she said aloud. 'Perhaps more than one person. Margaret Drue did not walk into the room on dead feet.' Bringing a head with her, but this Charmian did not say aloud, and secreted on her body a message to Charmian.

How did our paths cross? she asked herself. Did I see her one day? Not something I remember. But I meant something to her.

Emily stretched out a hand and gripped Charmian's wrist. 'Save me. Think about the past. Remember something. Save me.'

As they walked away, Jim Towers made his

52

own ironic comment. 'Save us, think about the past. Well, you might do that, ma'am. Try to remember where Margaret Drue met you.'

CHAPTER THREE

Charmian had plenty to think about as she walked away from Emily's flat. She had refused the drive home offered by Inspector Jim Towers.

'Save us,' he had said ironically, immediately the door closed behind them, 'Lives in a slum, doesn't she? And one of her own making. Save us. Think about the past. That's her advice, if you can call it that.' His voice was cold.

'I don't think there's much money.' Charmian decided to be cautious because there was a passion rolling through this man that ought to be moderated. 'It was save me, she said. I don't think she was much worried about you.'

'Thought that myself,' he said, suddenly giving a grin and at once becoming younger and less tense. 'Can't blame her, poor kid. Not going to be good for her whichever way you look at it ... Must have been her sister or her father that killed the child if it wasn't Drue.'

'You think so?'

'I do. And more to the point, so does HG.'

He held the door of the car open. 'Sure you won't take a lift?'

'I feel like walking.' And thinking. She did a lot of thinking when she was walking.

'What do you make of her?'

'Emily? Difficult to say, I don't know her that well, hard to know. A bit friendless.' She thought about it. 'Too much coffee and not enough food, it's the way students are.'

'She hasn't had much of a life, that girl.'

'I suppose not.' And then there was the other girl, the child who survived, whom he did not mention but whom Charmian remembered. Clara Meldrum, was she called?

'Take it from me, you don't when you are dragging that sort of thing behind you.'

'You could do with a trip to the past yourself. You found the child.'

'I never forget it. Wasn't my first body; that was a suicide in the Thames at Datchet, but it was the first child. I've seen other deaths by violence: one of the Cheasey little men (there was a group of very short families in Cheasey) was strangled by his brother, that wasn't nice. Then a stabbing in Merrywick ... you were in on that, ma'am.' Charmian nodded, so she had been. 'But the child was the first and the worst. Headless ... Well, now we've got the head,' Standing by the car door, he clenched his hands, opening and shutting the fingers. 'And I'd give anything to remember something valuable, any little thing, and I can't. I can't

54

remember a thing.'

'I don't know what I can do, but if I can remember anything about meeting Margaret Drue or even hearing about her, then you shall know. If you think it important.'

'Anything, anything.' He got in the car. 'Sure I can't drive you anywhere?'

To Dolly, you mean? No, we are lunching together and alone. But she took pity on him: 'We've got things to talk over. Dolly's still getting to terms with Kate's death. So am I. We both loved her.'

'I wish I had met her. I've heard what Dolly had to say about her. A blessed girl.'

It was a good and unexpected phrase from him. And it was all he had to say on the subject. He gave a kind of half-bow to signify that he was going, but meant to go politely, got into his car and drove away.

*   *   *

Dolly was waiting for her at the Fisherman's Bar with a glass of dry with wine. She seemed more cheerful. 'I like it here. My idea of what a pub should be. Everything genuine but the name, surely it started out as something else?'

Charmian looked around her at the quiet, dark, warm room. 'Yes, it's resisted the temptation to call itself the Dog and His Dinner and go chintzy and brassy with gas logs.' The fire, such as it was, smouldering away within a mask of smoke, was genuine. 'I believe it was originally called the Duke of Wellington.' And since there had probably been a pub or ale house here since William the Conqueror, no doubt it had been the Duke of Marlborough before that and the Great Harry before that, back to a nameless village ale house well known to the compilers of the Domesday Book.

Neither of them mentioned Kate, but she was there in the background of their conversation all the time. Kate had never, as far as either of them knew, come to this pub, which was why they came here now: there was no ghost of a tall and lovely girl to confound them with grief.

'How was Em?'

Charmian considered. 'Fraught.'

'Can't blame her. I'd be the same.'

'No, you wouldn't.' Charmian looked at her young friend. 'You've got what's called bottle. Otherwise, you wouldn't have taken up the career you have. She's anorexic too, I think.'

'Is she? What did Jim Towers think?'

Charmian shrugged. 'Not sure. Sorry for her, I think.'

Dolly drank some wine and eyed Charmian. 'You don't like Jim, do you?'

'Did I say that?'

'You don't have to.' Dolly finished her wine, putting down her glass with a defiant flourish.

'I do like him.' Suddenly she found herself

saying exactly what she felt: 'But I'd prefer him not to be so keen on heads.' Before Dolly could answer, to stop any reaction hitting her, she went on: 'How did you get to know Emily? I met her at a party you gave and she kind of clove to me. I liked her but there's the generation thing. How did you know her?'

The answer surprised her. 'Through Kate.'

'I wouldn't have expected them to be friends.'

'I don't know that they were. I liked Em more than Kate did, they weren't soul mates, but Anny knew Em's sister, she may even have known their mother, I believe she did, so the relationship goes a long way back. Not close though, there was an age difference.'

'I've already noticed that Emily seems to have no friends of her own age.'

'Oh, I expect she has,' said Dolly easily. 'She just keeps quiet about them, circles not mixing and that.'

Charmian looked out of the window, where you could just see the Thames, gleaming in the wintry sunlight. Anny Cooper had been her friend almost all her adult life. 'Odd that Anny never mentioned knowing the Baileys.'

'Never?'

'Never. I would have remembered.' Anny was a great talker as a rule, added to which she was very often engaged in a furious argument about something with someone, which she was willing to share with those of her friends who

57

would listen. No, Anny was not a silent lady.

'Did you mention that you knew Emily? Or that you were interested in the murder of ten years ago?'

'No, probably not. Anny didn't like hearing about my work, not since that murder which came so close home to her.' A friend and neighbour of Anny had been a particularly savage killer. That was in the past, but Anny had not forgotten, nor Charmian's part in it all. Also, Anny was in a confusion of grief at the death of her daughter and elation at the possession of a grandchild. Come to think of it, Anny had been at the party where she had met Emily Bailey. They had driven there together.

'I wonder if Anny knew Margaret Drue. Did you?'

Dolly shook her head. 'If I ever met her, then I don't remember. I used to visit Windsor, but I wasn't based here. Really, all I know is hearsay.'

'A lot of detection is hearsay,' said Charmian. 'I'll listen to anything you have.'

Dolly watched as a car arrived and a party of new lunchers arrived. Two men, two women, they were laughing. One woman was blonde and fat, but beautifully dressed. The other was small and dark, not so well dressed, but she was doing most of the laughing. Dolly recognized her as someone she had seen on television, a well-known actress. She watched for a moment, interested to see how different the

58

actress looked off screen without the make-up and clothes. The same yet different.

Then she turned back to Charmian. 'I do remember something, although it may not mean anything, just the sort of thing people say when there's this kind of tragedy. There was a low-key story that there was something odd, unpleasant going on at the school.'

'What sort of thing?' Charmian thought she could guess.

'Sex came into it somewhere.' Dolly pursed her lips. 'Nothing specific but there was the hint of child abuse.'

'Who told you?'

'I'm trying to remember ... I think I got it from the woman who sold newspapers outside the office I worked in ... She knew all the gossip. I didn't rate it very much; I never really believed all she said. Just took it in and shrugged. I don't think I believed it.'

'Is she still around, this newspaper-seller?'

Dolly looked sad. 'No, she died. Cancer. Such a nice old woman too.' She started to get herself together to depart. 'Must get back to work. Thanks for the drink and sandwich ... About the tale, the police team must have picked it up. Nothing got in the papers that I know of, but I expect they heard.'

'Be surprising if they hadn't.'

They parted in the car park. 'That was Amanda Royal, did you notice? The actress, I saw her arrive, and she came into the bar. I

59

heard her order a beef sandwich.'

'She is human; she eats.'

'But she does that TV advert about the green world and animals and eating vegetarian meals.' Dolly sounded shocked.

'That's work, this is her pleasure.' What a puritan Dolly could be.

As Dolly started the car, she leaned out of the window to wave goodbye. Her hair looked beautifully cut, shining and free.

'Who cuts your hair, Dolly?' called Charmian.

'Your friend Beryl Barker ... you sent me to her, she cuts well, you said, but watch her.' She waved again and was away.

Beryl Barker, Baby, an old friend, a good hairdresser but she could be dangerous company with a criminal past. But Dolly was streetwise and clever, she had certainly checked up on Baby. Charmian put a hand up to her own hair, which felt rough and dry. She might pop into Baby's herself.

On the edge of her mind, as if she was seeing it out of the corner of her eye, came a picture of wispy, floating hair going grey and a striped skirt in orange rather than yellow: Emily had said that everyone was wearing striped cotton skirts that summer. It was a shadow, a picture of a moment, then gone. Was that what Margaret Drue had looked like?

She smoothed her own hair: she would go to see Baby. There was one thing about Beryl

Andrea Barker, lawless she might be but she had great common sense. But one other thing first, even before her hair.

Charmian went straight back to her office, where she ignored the freshly arrived files on new cases (all of which she had asked for and truly needed to see), and the pile of letters demanding attention, in favour of telephoning Jim Towers.

He was at his desk, which surprised her somewhat since she had taken him for an out on the street, hands on investigation man, but he answered her politely, which did not surprise her. He would always be polite.

He also sounded hopeful, a hope she had to disabuse. 'No, I haven't got anything for you on Margaret Drue, I want to ask you something. Was there any suggestion of child abuse in the school?'

There was a perceptible pause. 'It was thought of, of course. I've checked the files, the case was kept open, but there was no evidence of it. It's clear that tactful enquiries were made and got nowhere, so that the idea was written off ... All the same...' She could hear him clearing his throat. 'I've talked to those men who worked on the case and are still around and each one said that they were troubled, and that they felt there was something, couldn't put their finger on it, they just smelt it.'

'What did it smell like?'

'Sex.' He was blunt. 'Somewhere, somehow.'

'I feel that too. It has to be somehow. But was anything ever discovered for sure?'

'They tried, believe me. That was what Drue was suspected of. Especially when she went missing. Now we know she was killed herself. I don't know if that clears her. To my mind it doesn't.'

'What state was the child's body in? Remind me.'

'She hadn't been physically abused, if that's what you mean. No sign of that at all.'

Charmian said: 'But there are ways of abusing children that are not always physical.'

'Some of the worst are, but it usually goes with a bit of knocking about too.' There was a question in his voice.

'Not sure exactly what I mean myself. Talking to the child, showing her pictures, letting her see scenes . . .' It wasn't nice what she was describing, but it could happen. 'And the child might talk about it.'

'Drue was the suspect, and may have been abusing the child in some way or the other. She may indeed have been the murderer of that child. And she may have been killed by another person in that household as an act of justice.'

'Do you think that?'

He was silent. 'No. It's so very brutal, the way the head and Drue's body were stuck together in that cupboard . . . Not justice, an act darker than that.'

'The head, you mean?'

'Not just the head. The whole feel of that cupboard and what was in it.'

'And that was why she was killed? Of course, it was always on the cards that the child was killed because of something she knew, but it was only speculative. Is still,' he said. 'No evidence, one way or the other. In the end I think the general feeling was it was just brutality: someone wanted to kill her.'

'There was brutality, all right, but something more as well.' Charmian was still puzzled, but so many years had now past since that killing, perhaps they would never get to the bottom of it all.

Not her affair, really. Or was it?

For somehow or other, Margaret Drue had dragged her into it.

*   *   *

At Anny's smart duplex apartment in a courtyard off Peascod Street, there was no sign of a baby in the airy cool establishment, unlike in some houses. This was because the whole upper floor, reached by its own lift, had been made over to the child, so that where Anny lived there was no smell of soap, talcum powder or nappies, no pram to see. Money could talk.

Anny's husband Jack was moping around the hall when Charmian arrived. He complained, 'I love the child, I'd be delighted to see the little scrap, push the pram.'

With two nurses? But Charmian did not say this aloud.

Anyway, Jack answered it. 'It's like getting to see the Queen. Worse, really. I have to wash my hands in disinfectant and take off my shoes.'

Charmian was not sure if she believed this. Jack in drink, as he was now, did tell tales. You couldn't help liking him, though. Drunk or sober, he was a good sort. The heart was there.

'Where's Anny?'

'She's not with the child.' He looked around as if he might see her, then shrugged. 'Considering she worships the kid, she sees very little of it.'

'Really?' It was hard with Jack when in this mood to know whether he spoke the truth or not.

'Ask her yourself, here she is.' He nodded towards the door.

Anny was there, Usually dressed in a trouser suit, but one that you knew came from a good couture house, possibly a French one—she had just come back from France; her arms were full of parcels which she let slip to the floor as she threw open her arms. 'Charmian, darling.'

So I am in favour? And Charmian responded herself. 'Anny love, I've come to see the baby.'

'Yes, go and see the little tyke,' said Jack from behind them.

Anny sighed. 'Sometimes, I think he doesn't know her sex. She's a girl, dear, a girl, sitting up and looking pretty.'

'Nearly sitting up,' said Jack. 'Fell over backwards last time I looked.'

'Can I go and see? Take a look?' You did not invade the nursery without permission. It had taken Charmian some time to recognize the rules of visiting but she was getting to know them now. And the first one was that you asked Anny. Who quite often said NO.

But she was in a good mood. 'Come on up.' She turned to Jack. 'Coming too, Grandpa?'

Jack looked visibly taken aback, even shocked, but although it would eat into valuable drinking time, which usually counted with him, he nodded. Speech seemed beyond him.

They all crowded into the lift, which rose swiftly to the top floor. Anny had decorated the walls with murals of her own. Not specially nursery stuff, but gay and lively. Also gentler than some of her latest production. She was abandoning the abstract, Charmian noticed, as were so many of her contemporaries, but there was a kind of idealized style to the landscapes she had painted over all the surface. The sun shone on fields and meadows while the full moon lit up a city street.

Peascod Street and Wellington Place, Charmian recognized with surprised pleasure. 'It's lovely, Anny.'

'Yes, some of my best work,' she said in a detached voice. 'I've backed it, you see, so I can remove it when I want.'

That was like Anny: she did not waste her work. The murals would go into an exhibition here or in America sooner or later, with a price on them, and if it was met, she would sell. Art was not about sentiment. This was something that Jack, a highly emotional man, had never understood, and it probably lay behind their worst quarrels.

One nurse was ironing something soft and white by the window; she nodded in welcome but worked on. This was Nurse Number Two. Number One Nurse was out, probably shopping for all the equipment the child seemed to need.

The baby was sitting in her play-pen, propped against a giant teddy bear whose eyes she was attacking with probing fingers; she was wearing a smocked blue silk dress and her hair was well brushed. She looked jocund, blithe and debonair.

So far unchristened, she was not unnamed: she was another Kate. Charmian found that very sad.

'She gets more like her mother every day,' said Anny.

'And her father.' Someone had to remember Rewley, who so often seemed to forget himself these days. And in fact the child already had a way of looking at you that was like Rewley's.

66

But she did have Kate's lovely hair and big blue eyes.

'I let him in occasionally, you know.' Anny looked without expression at Charmian, who supposed it was a joke, but grasped that it almost was but not quite. 'As much as he seems able to cope with. And Dolly Barstow. Why don't you find him some work to do to occupy his mind?'

Charmian stroked the baby's soft cheek. The thought was hard to handle but here it came: I could not call her Kate, not yet, perhaps not ever. 'It's work I came to you about.'

'Somehow I thought as much.'

Jack had sat himself down on the floor where he sat staring quietly, but she thought, happily at his grandchild. She stared back, giving the teddy bear a rest. It looked touch and go whether she smiled at Jack or burst into tears. She decided to smile. And the smile, when it came, was all her own, in it she resembled neither Kate nor Rewley.

But my God, Charmian thought, it's Jack. He smiled too and smile for smile seemed to match. But the baby who was not yet to be called Kate had added her own something to it, something feminine and delicate.

'I am occupied.' Yes, that was the word. 'I am occupied with the bodies in the old school house in Flanders Street. You've heard about them?'

'Who hasn't?'

'You knew Nancy?'

'Sure. You know I did, she was well known in Windsor. Everyone knew her. Before and after death.'

'What does that mean?'

'It means the Nancy after the body of the child was found and the school closed was not the one who later worked in the Castle. That one was a kind of zombie.'

Jack muttered: 'Don't talk about this sort of thing in the nursery in front of the baby.'

'She can't understand.'

'You can't be sure. You don't know how much babies take in.'

Anny shrugged. 'If ancestry has anything to do with it, then she must be used to it, crime talk bred in the bone.'

This was Anny being at her worst, Charmian wished she had not come.

'Did you know Margaret Drue?'

'Yes, to that too.' Anny turned her head. 'You did too, Jack, didn't you?'

'Don't remember.'

'One of Jack's drinking companions of those years.'

'She was not.'

Anny said: 'So she's turned up in the house, dead?'

'Looks like it,' Charmian said cautiously.

'Nancy was a friend, I knew Margaret Drue through her, she brought Margaret to one of my exhibitions and she made some sensible

68

observations. Not a nice woman but she didn't deserve to be murdered. Still, I suppose it's marginally better than being thought to be a murderer.'

'Did you ever mention my name?'

'To Margaret Drue?' Anny was surprised now. 'I hardly spoke to her. She wasn't one of my favourite people. We were polite to each other when we met, you know how one does in Windsor, but I never mentioned you as far as I know. Why?'

'It doesn't matter.'

'Clearly it does.' Anny was trying to help now. 'Ask Jack, he may have done. No, I don't mean that nastily, Jack. The woman was your friend, even if I didn't like her. You may have talked of Charmian.'

'Don't remember,' said Jack. He stood up, moving away from the baby.

'All right.' Anny patted him on the arm. 'She was a nicer woman than I admit, a good friend to you, and I am a jealous cow. Or was. I hope there is no need for that now, Jack?'

'Certainly not,' said Jack stiffly, who to do him justice, as Charmian sometimes did, was a great drunk and wanderer but not unfaithful. Or not lately.

The nurse came over, picked up the child and said: 'Going for our lovely walk now ... We're going to the park, Granny.'

'Right. I ordered the fruit you wanted, it will all be delivered.'

'Do you want any help carrying the child down?' This was Jack.

'No, thank you, Mr Cooper, we have to have a wash and tidy first and I can manage beautifully in the lift.'

Jack wasn't Grandpa to the nurse, Charmian noticed, as she thought he did too, and even Anny had seemed to use the name more as a weapon. Life was sometimes very unfair to Jack.

'Come on then,' ordered Anny. 'Let's go into the studio and have a drink. Jack can mix us a martini.'

'It's the middle of the afternoon,' protested Charmian.

'You used to drink in the afternoon.'

'That was then.'

But Jack made no martinis, disappearing no doubt to some private toping of his own, and the two women drank tea. Anny showed Charmian her latest paintings.

'They're good,' Charmian appraised. 'Really good, and different.' Not exactly gentler, but quieter.

'I know.' Anny always accepted praise without fuss. 'For a time, I couldn't work, but now I've begun again.' She looked at her friend speculatively, wondering, as they all did, how her marriage was working and if she was happy. It was hard to associate Charmian with total, perfect happiness.

Charmian put down her cup. 'I'll tell you
70

why I wanted to ask about Margaret Drue, it's not particularly secret, not as far as I am concerned. She had a newspaper cutting about me, tucked inside her clothing. Cut from a local paper and dating from the time I came here to give a talk just before I took up my previous position.'

'Yes, that is strange.' Anny poured some more tea. 'Hidden? As if it was a secret?'

'Something like that ... she had a message asking me for help scrawled on it.'

Anny thought about it for a moment, then her real affection for her friend showed through. 'I don't like it for you.'

'I don't think I'm in any personal danger. But why my name came into her mind...' Charmian shrugged. 'I suppose it could have been Jack. There was that local murder I was involved with, it would have been in his mind.' Except who knew what was in Jack's mind?

'Jack had nothing to do with the death or what went on in the school.'

'No, of course not. I never thought so for a minute.'

'Yes, you did. Passed through your mind. You looked at the idea.'

Charmian laughed. 'You devil, Anny. Well, perhaps a notion flashed through, but no, not Jack.'

He knew something though, she had read it in his face. Not guilt but knowledge.

She finished her tea. 'I'm off. Let me know if

I can do anything. And don't forget Rewley is the child's father. I'm back to work.'

'He comes round, but he couldn't possibly look after the child.'

'Perhaps he ought to be allowed to try.'

Anny became serious. 'Listen to me, I know what I'm talking about. You've never had a child, you can't put them out for the day like a kitten. This baby is a full-time job.'

'For three women?' asked Charmian.

'I'll ignore that. No, I won't. Yes, he could have the nurses, Kate's trust fund which is now for the use of her child could pay for what was needed, since I don't suppose the salary of a serving officer could run to it, but Rewley hasn't got the emotional strength at the moment. He's still living in the shadows.'

Charmian was silent: she could not deny it. George Rewley had withdrawn to a world of his own.

'What you can do,' Anny swept on, 'is to see he gets back to work. Work is what he needs now. Don't worry, he can have the child when he wants.'

'Sorry, Anny. I should have trusted you more.'

'For my oldest friend, you make a good critic,' said Anny without rancour. 'Come on, I'll see you out. Let me know how the investigation goes. As a case it makes my flesh creep.'

Mine too, thought Charmian.

Anny walked through the open courtyard of Wellington Place, of which she was now the owner, having absorbed the other apartments into her domain. 'The nannies have to live somewhere, we can't all pig in together,' she had said blithely, 'and I am constructing a small gallery for shows.'

Geraniums in great pots and a fuschia tree stood about; Anny patted them as she walked past. The entrance to the court now had an iron grille for security and privacy, but Charmian had parked round the corner, probably illegally, but her car was known and it was one of the few ways in which she exploited her position.

Jack was sitting in her car in the passenger seat. 'You ought to have locked your car.'

'I know.' She got in the car to sit beside him. 'Come on, Jack, what is it? Want me to drive you anywhere?'

'I wanted to say that I did tell Margaret Drue about you. I did not give her the cutting or even tell her about it, I didn't see her after the child's body was found, she disappeared, this was before.'

'You talked about me. Why, Jack? Any special reason? Not just because you liked my face.'

'Always admired you, Charmian.' Jack stared straight ahead. 'But the woman was worried. She was trying to drop her past, be good, not easy, you know.' Jack knew all about

73

struggling to mend your ways. 'She knew something about the school that she didn't like.'

'She was suspected of killing the child.'

'I know, and when she disappeared, then I was worried too. Didn't know what to think or what to say. You weren't here then or I might have talked to you. Anny and I were having one of our non-talkers. You know...'

'I know.' Non-talkers were when Jack cleared off, disappeared you could say, and drank his way into oblivion before returning, when life between Anny and Jack would resume. It seemed a terrible kind of therapy for him. He hadn't behaved like this lately.

'So I decided Margaret had done in the kid and cleared off. She was a strange lady. Of course, I didn't know about her record, no one did, the school should have done, but didn't.'

'You're talking too much, Jack.'

'The rumour going round the town is that she was murdered herself. Which makes her innocent.' He sounded troubled.

'That seems to be what happened. But we don't know how or why, Jack. She may have been killed in revenge because she did kill the child.'

He looked even more troubled. 'Do you believe that?'

'It's a possibility.'

'Proper copper, aren't you?' There was a touch of bitterness in his voice. 'Dead, killed, murdered, and still you're measuring her up for a crime.'

Charmian was silent, then: 'Say what you have to say, Jack, and get on with it.'

'All I know is, she said something rotten was going on in that school.'

'Any details? Names? What she meant?'

'Sex,' he said. 'Had to be from the way she spoke and the look in her eyes. She wasn't a totally nice woman, but better than they say, and I'd learnt to read her. She knew something, and I reckon she was killed because of it.' He started to get out of the car. 'I feel I owe her.'

'If she didn't do the killing first. She had a record. What was it she said to you?'

'She said: there's some sex game going on among those kids.'

'Exact words, Jack?'

'Exact words.'

'And was this before or after you talked about me?'

'Kind of in the middle. What she had to say came out in dribs and drabs. Until that last sentence, and she said that quick and fast.'

'Were you in bed with her at the time, Jack?'

'I was not,' he said with some dignity.

He stood on the kerb's edge watching as Charmian started the car. 'All right, Jack, you've said it.'

'Sorry I mentioned your name to her.'

'Forget it. You may have done the right thing.'

75

She began to drive, leaving him standing on the kerb looking lost. It was his badge, that look. He had been born with it but years of marriage to Anny had put a polish on it. The marriage held, though, and was even enjoyed in its odd way by both parties.

As she gave one last look behind her, she saw his face; it was full of pain. The thought came to her: Jack is in this murk deeper than you think. Damn you, Jack. I like you, you are married to my oldest friend, and the father of my godchild, I want you in the clear.

She stopped the car, wound down the window and called out over her shoulder: 'I'll be in touch, Jack.' Then drove off. Let him make of that what he liked.

It looked as though Jack was responsible for introducing her name to Margaret Drue. Oh Margaret Drue, she apotheosized as she drove away. What were you and why did you use my name? Or did you? Perhaps someone else, your killer maybe, put that piece of paper in your bra. In that case, whose was the cry for help?

And were you an innocent victim of the person who had killed the child? Or were you the child killer yourself, executed for your crime? And if so, who was your executioner?

And the head of the child? What did that mean? Too many questions.

The head had been found, and then placed between the knees of a dead woman.

I don't like this introduction of the head. It's

76

like a terrible parody of a virgin and child. She drove on smartly. I'll put that to Jim Towers to see what he thinks ... 'Jim,' she might say, 'how does the head of Alana fit into your catalogue of heads? A memento mori, a symbol of revenge, or a present from the past?'

There was one other person who had known Charmian in those early days in Windsor when Margaret Drue had heard her name, a person moreover who took a professional interest in heads. This was Beryl Andrea Barker, Baby to her friends, of whom Charmian must now be counted as one, although she had at one time been responsible for sending Baby to prison for a long term.

And would again, if required, she told herself firmly. But Baby had reformed, and now ran a successful hairdressing establishment in Meadow Street, Windsor, as well as another in Merrywick. The days when she had been an active member of a gang of women criminals were long past. Nor regretted by her. 'And it was not like they make it out on the telly, dear,' she had once explained to Charmian, 'it was drear.'

Meadow Street was on the edge of Windsor in an area once unsmart but steadily becoming gentrified and more expensive. Miss Barker (she refused to be Ms, saying her unmarried state was important to her) had moved her establishment here within the last year because it offered her larger premises and excellent

77

parking. Charmian saw that the outside had been repainted a brighter pink (Baby loved pink) since her last visit and deduced that confidence was high.

The door was opened by Baby herself, a crest of golden curls in which a blue chiffon scarf was artfully twined topped her head; a minimal blue silk skirt and a matching shirt gave Charmian an idea of her mood: upbeat. Baby in a bad low state wore distressed jeans and a cotton shirt.

Over the years a quiet friendship had grown up between the two women, together with a certain respect. Charmian valued Baby's sharp view of the world and Baby for her part trusted the honesty of her friend. On the matter of fashion, the differences were stronger, with Baby shrugging her shoulders at her friend's conservative taste while she herself liked to wear strong, bright, expendable clothes. Buy today, wear tomorrow, throw away the day after, that was her credo.

'There you are, and not before time.' She ran her fingers through Charmian's hair. 'Let me get my razor.'

'Just trimmed and washed,' pleaded Charmian.

Baby gave another appraising look: 'And you could do with a tint, the roots are showing.'

'Thanks. You are making me feel good.'

'The truth is always best,' said Baby

virtuously. Then she caught sight of her friend's raised eyebrows. 'As far as looks are concerned, I'm not saying of life in general.'

Baby had been a fluent and unembarrassed liar to the police and in court in what she called 'the old days', and had not lost the gift.

'Well, that was business,' she said, reading Charmian's face. 'And you're a friend, I don't lie to you.'

Charmian sat down. 'I'll have a blow dry if you will do it yourself.' Baby only attended to the hair of favoured clients, who were charged twice the normal rate for the privilege.

'Want to talk, do you?' asked Baby, handing over a robe, and seating Charmian.

'What makes you say that?'

'I can read you like a book.'

The razor appeared and was sent swooping over Charmian's head. 'Don't take too much off,' she pleaded. 'Humphrey doesn't like it shorn.'

'Oh yes,' Baby's hand hovered. 'How's that going?'

'Very well, thank you.'

'Tricky business being married, especially for the second time. It is your second, and not the third?' said Baby sagely. 'Wouldn't risk it myself.' She lowered the razor. 'Nasty business you've got down in Flanders Street. An unlucky name, I've said so before. I nearly bought a house there when I first came to Windsor, but no, I said, that name is associated

79

with death. And I wasn't wrong, was I?'

Charmian would have answered but Baby had her head pressed down like a dog she was grooming.

'No,' she managed, as she got her head up and could breathe again. 'You were living here when the child Alana was missing.'

'Murdered, you mean.' She was finishing the cut with scissors which gave a sharp snip. 'Say what you mean. Yes, I was.' The scissors hovered. 'But I can't help you there. I did Miss Bailey's hair once or twice but that was all. Lovely hair, she had, but neglected. Not what I'd call a looker but she could have made something of herself if she'd tried. Other things on her mind, I suppose.' After a while she stood back. 'I think I've got you right. Just lightened you a touch. You need lightening . . . Of course, she never came back after the murder.' Baby was brushing the hair from Charmian's neck and shoulders. 'And I remember not being surprised about the murder.' She frowned. 'I wonder why that was? Someone must have told me something. You hear all sorts of gossip here from under the dryer. Sometimes not true.'

'Was there talk about the school?'

Baby looked thoughtful as she led Charmian to a wash basin, motioning to an assistant to come forward. There was a class structure in her salon by which only juniors washed hair.

'Talk about the school as such or about people?'

80

'Can't remember.' Baby had her eye on the girl assistant. 'Not too much shampoo and only one wash, then conditioner,' she ordered. 'Your hair is so dry. Out of condition, you ought to watch it ... You can't separate the school from the people, can you?'

A shower of water and strong hands rubbing her scalp kept Charmian quiet for a minute until she could escape. Dabbing her eyes, she saw that Baby was still by her side.

'That's enough, Julie. Madam's done now. Towel, please.'

'Did you know one of the teachers, Margaret Drue?'

Baby paused. 'That's quite a question, isn't it? She was the one who was supposed to have done it, wasn't she? And now her body has been found in the house. It was on the TV news. Pictures as well. Yes, she came here sometimes. Her hair wasn't much and she didn't take care of it.'

'What did you make of her?'

'I'll have to think about that,' said Baby. 'Why?'

'Did you ever mention my name to her?'

'I don't talk about you all the time,' said Baby smartly. 'In fact, come to think of it, hardly any of the time.'

Charmian knew that evasive talk. 'Did you?'

Baby drew a breath. 'I recognized her, I'd seen her before, we were in the same nick for a bit.'

81

'I see.' Presumably the police had discovered this fact, and thought it not significant. 'And did she recognize you?'

'No. And I can tell you we didn't talk about the police in any shape or form. In fact, I kept out of her way.'

'You didn't want to be claimed as a friend?'

'I knew what she'd been in for: touching up a kid. More than one, probably.'

'Weren't you surprised that she was teaching in a school?'

'No, it's the sort of place a person like her would head for ... anyway, I didn't know then where she was working, not till afterwards. What is all this?'

'She used my name ... she seemed to think I could help her.'

'She'd have been wrong then, wouldn't she? You're not into helping that sort.'

Charmian did not answer but Baby went on talking. 'She's dead now, and innocent of the killing.'

Did she really believe this? Possibly, Charmian thought, but I am reserving judgement.

'But I'll tell you about her: she was S.I.M.— that's the phrase, isn't it?—Strange in Manner. Not all the time, but now and then. Flashes of oddness. I suppose she controlled it at the school but she let it get out sometimes.'

Like an animal that had to be fed, thought Charmian with a shudder.

82

'And that's when she was having bad thoughts,' said Baby. 'You know what I mean.'

Charmian looked at her reflection in the looking-glass above the basin and saw Baby's expression.

'If I'd been a child and I'd seen that look, I'd have run a mile. Perhaps that kid did. Only not fast enough.'

As Charmian paid her bill, she could hear herself saying to Jim Towers: I've tracked several people who knew me and from whom Margaret Drue might have got the idea of calling on me for help. She didn't have to know, or even see me, but she knew my name and general character. I can be sure of that. And I have the idea that she was killed because she had abused and murdered Alana. So you will have to look for a revenge killer.

Baby said: 'Come out of that dream, I'm talking to you . . .'

'I'm listening.'

'You'd better . . . I had a friend of yours in here earlier in the week . . . Miss Eagle, she knows I know you and we often chat about you, I was doing her hair . . . well, her wig really.'

Charmian was diverted. 'I didn't know she had a wig.'

'Oh it's not a secret, I've washed it before. Bright red. She doesn't wear it all the time, she says it's for ceremonial purposes.'

Winifred Eagle and Birdie Peacock were

friends and neighbours of Charmian in Maid of Honour Row where they shared a house round the corner from her. They were ladies of late middle age, but ageless as they said themselves, who practised a variety of white magic. They were friendly, charming witches of great kindness and equal eccentricity. 'We are experimental with life,' Winifred had said once to Charmian, who thought it an understatement. She admired them and was close to loving them for their generosity and integrity.

She found herself wondering what the ceremony was for which the wig was required. Some carnal spring festival, perhaps. Winifred, although of great respectability in everyday life, was not inhibited in her religious or wiccer practices. Neither was Birdie, who celebrated nakedness with relish.

'We were talking about the discovery of the body. There's been a lot of talk, because all the locals remember the school and the Baileys, the girl Emily is still around. I don't know her myself but her name came up as being still here. Talk, you see. There's not been much detail in the papers but everyone's been naming names and Drue was certainly top of the list. And there's talk about a head being found?' Baby looked at Charmian. 'Well, you're keeping quiet like you usually do, but there was a head, wasn't there?'

Charmian nodded.

'I was dressing the wig on one of those

wooden heads and that was how the subject came up; Miss Eagle had heard about the head and she said she'd like to talk to you about it, hadn't seen much of you lately since your marriage. Heads were important, she said, and I agree.'

Charmian nodded. You, Winifred Eagle and Jim Towers. 'I'll look in.'

At the door, the last thing Baby said, as if she had been saving it up: 'She wondered if the head had been boiled.'

A thought to leave you with. Charmian thought about it as she sat in her car. It was due time to visit Birdie and Winifred to pay the dog's bill. Her dog Benjy lived with the white witches whose company and garden he preferred, but Charmian underwrote his expenditure, which, since he was accident prone and a big eater, was not small either in dog food or at the local veterinary surgery where he was known as Big Ben.

She drove round there now, parking her car outside her own house and walking round the corner. Benjy was in the garden, he began to bark with enthusiasm when he saw her; he never forgot her, although Charmian sometimes wished he would.

Birdie put her head out of the window. 'It's Charmian, dear,' she called back to Winifred.

The front door opened, Winifred held out a welcoming hand. She was the plumper of the two women, usually the more conventionally dressed in a tweed suit and woolly shirt, whereas Birdie was wilder and colourful. Where Birdie got her clothes was a mystery; it may be she made them herself because her sweep of silk and brocade was often pinned and stuck together. Once a particular confection of gauze and chiffon had collapsed altogether, revealing that Birdie wore nothing underneath. But that had been in a heatwave. Today was chilly and she wore a red woollen shift to counterpoint Winifred's brown and black check. Charmian felt wrongly dressed herself as she walked in, as if she was wearing camouflage and they were normal. She recognized that the witches were sending out strong thought-waves to which, alas, she was sometimes susceptible.

'Thought you might be round. You got my message?'

'Baby said something.' Charmian bent down to pat Benjy's head. From a high bookcase, the witches' black cat, Ben, looked down with big yellow eyes. It was thought he resented the fact that Benjy had a name which so much resembled his own; both of them answered to Ben which caused trouble at feeding time, except that the witches usually summoned the dog with the words 'Good Boy', which call he was happy to answer.

'Yes, I got the word.'

'I thought Birdie and I could be helpful,' said Winifred. She sounded grave. Her best witch's

86

voice. 'We knew the school, and the whole family, even Emily who was so much younger. You know the gossip was that she was really Nancy's child?'

'I didn't know that. Was it true?'

'I think it was. But who the father was, I could not guess. Perhaps the driver of the car in the accident in which Nancy was lamed. She limped badly. Did you know that?'

Charmian frowned. This sounded strange. 'I had heard about her leg.' Emily had told her.

'She was good at disguising it, but on occasion it showed.'

'How did it happen?'

Winifred shrugged. 'Opinions differ: it might have been the result of the accident, she wasn't born that way, she appeared that way after an absence, but she never explained and with her you learned not to ask. Years ago, of course, I hardly knew her then.' She went to a side table, 'Take a whisky?'

The witches whisked up herbal mixtures of amazing colours in the electric blender which they both drank themselves and pressed on their friends, but they made no secret of the belief that alcohol had its part to play and whisky was their preferred tipple, blended or a pale malt according to mood. Today, Winifred was offering a famous malt.

'I won't, thank you. What is it you were going to tell me?'

'Heads are important. I want you to know

that.'

Birdie said quietly, as she accepted whisky and added ice, 'Don't jump in, Win. You always go in with both feet.'

'Best to be straight, Birdie.'

'I know heads are important in murder cases, if that is what you are telling me.' Charmian kept her voice down. 'My last big case was one in which the body was in bits, as you very well know.'

'Yes, poor girl, that was awful, that was just for the convenience of the killer, but that's not what I am saying. There's a psychic element to the severed head. I think of the heads in the Ruxton killing long ago ... Dr Ruxton cut off the heads of the two women, and it was not just to prevent their identification.' She held up a hand. 'There was an element of that in it. Strands are mixed, but Jim Towers and I agree that there was something else. The same with the Cleveland serial murders...'

'Oh, so Inspector Towers comes into it?'

'He's interested in the way we are.'

Not quite, Charmian thought, you are two women and he is a serving police officer who has been interested in severed heads since he was first on the beat. Had his first direct experience. That builds up to a different picture in my mind.

'What you've got to remember is that the killer fears the heads. They say something, the dead see him. The eyes can identify him. The killers of PC Gutteridge pierced his eyes so that their faces would not be there for all to see. Frozen, fixed in the dead eyes.'

'You don't believe that. Nor does Jim Towers.'

'It was what the killers believe, in the unconscious mind, perhaps consciously sometimes. The head is dangerous magic.'

'So you think that was why the child's head was cut off?'

'Yes.' Winifred said it simply; Birdie nodded sagely over her glass of whisky. 'Say it for us both, old girl,' she said.

Charmian had a sudden moment of illumination. 'Did you know the child?'

'Yes.' Birdie answered this time. 'We both did.'

'Not well,' said Winifred, 'but we both used to meet her. I worked part-time in the library then, in the children's room, and Alana used to come in. She was only a little thing but her parents were abroad a good deal so that she then boarded in the holidays. So someone from the school would bring her out for a walk or shopping and once or twice a week to the library. She liked books even though she could only just read. She would be left bored, and she was only little, after all, we would talk. She was so bright, observant and inquisitive. I encouraged her in that.' Winifred looked at Charmian. 'I felt that I might have encouraged her to observe too much and perhaps that was

89

why she was killed.'

Charmian did not answer.

'Was a motive ever discovered? There wasn't one, was there?'

'So you think she saw or heard something which was why she was killed?'

'I did feel responsible. Not at the time, it seemed too nebulous, but the idea grew on me, especially since talking to Jim Towers.' She smiled at Charmian. 'I don't say I have felt guilty all these years, you know me better than that, but I have felt that I might have played a part.'

'I see.' And she did.

'And the head was significant, you see. A child's head, with eyes opened inquisitively, tongue speaking.'

Charmian stood up. Time had passed rapidly. 'I'd better get off. But thanks for telling me ... if you feel guilty, any guilt at all, and want to help, there is one other young creature in trouble. Would you help with Emily?'

'Yes.' But Winifred frowned, she needed to know more. 'Doing what?'

'Would you have her to stay? Just for a while, while the investigation gets under way. I don't think she ought to be on her own.'

Winifred and Birdie looked at each other. Then a nod passed between them.

'Yes,' said Winifred. 'She can go in the spare room. She'll have to look after herself a bit. Eat

90

what we eat, not mind when we are out.'

'A bit of company is what she needs.'

'Will you tell her, or shall I?'

'I will, I will telephone.' And she would get Dolly to back her up.

She drove back to her office, where she dialled Emily's number. She didn't have a line of her own, but there was a telephone in the hall outside her room and Charmian had noted the number.

A young male voice answered, and said yes, he would bang on her door. In a short while he was back: 'She's not in, she isn't in much, but she is usually home in the evening a bit later.' He seemed to know her movements. 'Shall I tell her you called?'

'No, I'll try again later.'

She telephoned her own home in Maid of Honour Row, but Humphrey was not yet back. They had an evening engagement in the Castle so she left a message saying that she would be back in time to change and go. Would he book a table for dinner afterwards?

She sat thinking, evaluating her day. Had it been a waste of time?

No, she had got a sense of what might have been happening in the deaths of Margaret Drue and the child Alana. The killer of the child and her victim, was that what they had in the cupboard? The head of the child accusatory of Margaret Drue and placed there for that reason? Then who was the self-appointed avenger, who did what a policeman could not or should not, actually kill? Are we accusing Jim Towers, she asked herself. What rubbish, stop it.

I suppose we are an evaluating outfit here, she argued to herself. I see all the records, check them and pass judgement. I am a kind of secret eye running over all crime cases in my jurisdiction, I have four investigators helping me: Dolly, Rewley, Nick and Jane, but I provide the power.

The telephone rang, interrupting her thoughts. Possibly it was Emily. Good, she wanted Emily in a kindly and watchful household. But to her surprise it was Rewley. She started to tell him she had seen his daughter, and how was he, and he must have as long a rest from work as he wanted. But he broke in: 'I have an informer. It relates to the finding of the body and the child's head. I want permission to use.' He didn't say him or her, unlike Rewley who was usually so open.

'Right, go ahead, you have my permission. Usual rules.'

'No money has passed between us, nor will just yet, but I will keep the rules.'

'Can you say anything, give me any details?' She always allowed her team to work without a nagging supervision from her, but this time she felt she would like to know more.

'I would rather not. Not yet.'

'I need to know something.'

There was a pause. 'My informant...' he hesitated.

'Go on. What does he say?'

'Did I say he?'

'He, she or it,' said Charmian irritably. 'Give me it.'

Rewley seemed to be speaking carefully. 'My informant spoke of human remains...'

She hesitated, then: 'OK, fine. Go ahead.' The conversation ended there, with no more talk between them. Rewley was back to work with a vengeance. Not perhaps the right word to use in this context, with revenge so much in her mind.

CHAPTER FOUR

Charmian went home to the house in Maid of Honour Row without having got in touch with Emily. But she had done one thing: she had driven past the house in Flanders Street where she saw a uniformed constable on guard. From the number of cars parked along the road, and the long black van at the end of the row of houses, she understood that Jim Towers had made this his Incident Room, at least for the time being.

She sat there thinking. Was she really coming to believe that a young police officer could have killed in revenge? No, not revenge, as an act of retribution because he had seen the dead child. It was a mad thought, surely not to be encouraged.

Just for a little while, she did encourage it: she liked Jim Towers but he aroused strong and worried reactions inside her. Was he an obsessive person who could kill? And if so, there were big questions.

Where had he got the head from? And how had he found it and how killed Margaret Drue? No, it was madness.

She sat watching because there was a lot going on around the black van. A uniformed constable arrived and walked in, followed by a woman police officer, neither of whom she recognized. Two men in plain clothes emerged and got into one of the cars and drove off; she didn't recognize them either. Then Jim Towers came down the steps of the van, on his own, and stood looking around before walking into the house.

Now what's up.

But he was out soon, striding towards his own car which was parked up the road. He sat for a minute, then drove off. He passed Charmian without noticing her. Well, good luck for you, she thought.

So she continued to drive home. Home is where the heart is, but she asked herself if her heart was really there or in her office. Which would make the office her true home. And this was what her enemies and some of her friends said. It was a hard word, but it might be a true one.

Yet when she got to Maid of Honour Row, her mood changed. The house felt warm and welcoming, Muff the cat observed her from a comfortable seat in the kitchen and Humphrey opened the door to her wearing the striped silk dressing-gown from Turnbull and Asser which had been her birthday present when she had not known him very long. Since she knew now that he really preferred his old woollen one which had seen long service, she took this kindly.

He went to the kitchen. 'Want a drink? I'm having one.'

She threw her coat over the table, which was clean, empty and tidy which was not how she had left it that morning, so Humphrey must have got to work. Nice to have a house-trained husband.

'No, thank you.' She kissed him. 'I've got a telephone call to make.'

No response from Emily. Even the helpful young man left the phone unanswered. It didn't mean that no one was there, it meant that no one was bothering. Let the phone ring, someone else's business. Emily herself might be there.

She came back to Humphrey. 'I'll have that drink now.' As he poured it, she said: 'Nice dressing-gown.'

'Yes,' he handed a cool long glass over. 'A

95

woman gave it me.'

'Forward creature.'

'I wanted her to be.'

They looked at each other. 'It wouldn't matter if we were late for this party,' she said.

'Not a bit.'

She picked up her drink. 'I'll bring my drink with me, it always tastes better in bed.'

Later, but not too much later, because there was this royal party, she said, head on the pillow: 'Do you ever have a wispy feeling about something, that is yet good and strong at the same time?'

He didn't quite understand her, but wanted to be helpful. 'Often,' he touched her bare shoulder, 'and it's usually about you.'

'This is about murder.' Not a nice thought in bed.

'I love you.'

'I know. It gets better, doesn't it? I thought marriage might make it boring...' she did not finish the sentence. 'I suppose we had better get up.'

But she did not move, and neither did he.

'Mustn't be later than the Queen.'

'She would understand.'

'Think so? We could hardly explain: Sorry, Ma'am, but we were otherwise occupied.'

*   *   *

They were late for the party but the Queen did

not notice. She was in a group of four, talking happily, and did not turn her head as they slid through the door.

'She noticed,' whispered Charmian. 'I believe she always does.'

Their hostess walked across to greet them. 'You're late.' Frivolous and light-hearted in many ways, Lady Mary took her duties seriously. Especially since she had recently married and was now Lady Mary Dalrymple; her husband was a serving soldier in a Highland regiment. No money, but a marvellous pedigree and lots of ambition. He was at present serving abroad. Lady Mary was tall, and beautiful in a straightforward English way with blue eyes and straight fair hair.

'Work,' pleaded Charmian, trusting her lie did not show.

'I know, I made your excuses. HM is interested in the case, she wants to talk to you.'

Charmian rolled her eyes. 'Surely not?'

'Have a drink first, you will need it, HM will put you through a close questioning. Better get rehearsed.' Lady Mary handed a glass of champagne to Charmian and whisky to Humphrey whom she knew well, and had indeed known longer than Charmian and had considered falling in love with him, only there was her soldier boy to whom her heart, if not always her body, had remained reluctantly faithful.

'She can't know much about it.' Charmian

97

sipped her champagne, appreciating what she had been given: Lady Mary always offered good drinks. She claimed to be poorer than ever since her marriage, but she had settled comfortably into her grace and favour apartment in the Castle, earned by some nameless appointment. Nothing about her looked like poverty—but it's all relative, Charmian told herself, she might miss the gold plate and the family diamonds.

'You'd be surprised what she knows. Reads everything.'

'You are not cheering me up.'

'Just warning you. What do you think, Humphrey?'

Humphrey answered calmly: 'I think you are doing this on purpose. Don't bait my wife.'

Lady Mary laughed. 'Still, she does want to know about the murders. She's interested, I am myself. I was in France at the time of the child's death, improving my French, so I didn't hear about it at first, but I knew Nancy afterwards when she used to drift around the place like a ghost. She was a ghost really, the school was her life, and when that went, she went with it.'

'What was she like?' Charmian was curious. 'I can't put together any clear picture from talking to the younger sister Emily.'

'I liked Nancy, what I knew of her, a gentle, kind woman. I never met the younger girl, but I gather she was a wild one, and as for her father...' Lady Mary shrugged. 'You hear

98

tales, a bit of a bully.'

'He shouldn't have been running a school for young children if he was like that,' said Humphrey.

'But he wasn't, it was Nancy's school.' Lady Mary always stood by her friends. 'There was a bit of talk that old man Bailey had done the killing; a lot of people wanted it to be him, it would have been kind of neat.'

And the police investigating team had hoped it was him too; Charmian had read the reports in the file on Alana's death, a file which was still open. But he had been proved to have been elsewhere at the time the child had died, or at least no one had been able to prove he had been anywhere near here. Nor was there any forensic evidence. In fact, forensics had not been helpful at all. There were traces of wood, fabric and paint on the child's clothing which did not seem to have come from the school, but with nothing and no one to match them against they had been of no value. Police regrets all round.

'No, it wasn't him,' she said aloud.

'And then, the Drue woman went missing and her past came out and she seemed the obvious person. It is true she's been found with the head of the girl? There have been all sorts of stories.'

'Something like that,' said Charmian in a neutral voice.

'Oh, don't give anything away, but it's

interesting. You can't blame HM. Do you think Drue was killed in revenge? But the head? How did that get there?'

'Someone put it there.'

'But where was it?'

Charmian shrugged. 'I don't know.'

Humphrey said: 'Perhaps Margaret Drue had it by her, Nielsen kept bits and pieces of bodies around him.'

Lady Mary moved away, aware that she had drained out what information she could. 'What a horrible picture you draw ... Now remember you will be summoned and be ready.'

'Do I curtsey?'

'No, we've all done that once as a body and yours will be taken as done, even HM likes to relax sometimes.' She moved away with easy graceful steps.

'Do you think she meant it? About the Queen, I mean?'

'I don't know, difficult to tell with our Mary. But you will soon find out.'

'The Queen's not looking my way.'

'It's not done like that. If you are wanted, you will be summoned.'

'Like Queen Victoria's chair,' said Charmian. 'I'll just be there.'

The room where Lady Mary was giving her party had great arched windows looking over an inner courtyard bordered with stone walls which looked as though they could withstand a siege. A long time since that had happened, even King John had preferred to ride out to Runnymede rather than face the barons here. The great fire of last autumn had not reached Lady Mary's apartments.

The room was not over-large but Lady Mary seemed to have filled it with handsome furniture and fine pictures. Presumably these were family stuff unless she had raided a museum. Or perhaps the Castle loaned them out to her? Heaven knows, from Charles I onwards they had been great collectors, and the cellars were reputed to be full of masterpieces which came out in turn.

The guests matched the furnishings, being not young and of the best quality. Perhaps it was obligatory in the royal presence, Charmian mused, for all the women to have the same sleek hair-style, well under control, and to have dresses of heavy silk from a good couture house, and a little jewellery but not too much. More latitude was allowed to the men in the matter of hair and beards, but a good tailor seemed necessary. Shirts too must follow certain rules as to colour and length of cuff, with which it was better to wear a regimental tie if you could claim one, as most of those here could do.

She gave Humphrey a quick look. Yes, he was following the rules. She ran an uneasy hand over her hair. She, alas, was not.

Humphrey touched her arm. 'You are about to be summoned.'

*   *   *

When she came back, she said to Humphrey: 'Well, she really wanted to talk about the difficulty of keeping horses in good form in bad weather. Most of that went to that man with a bald head standing next to her.'

'That's the Marquess of Anstruther, he breeds horses, breeds everything. Do you know he's got five sons and three daughters? Go on, didn't you get your turn?'

'Oh yes, HM said that at least two of her ancestors had been beheaded and she was interested in heads ... She said it was thought to be a noble way to die, reserved for upper-class prisoners. Better than hanging.'

'Granted the technical expertise of early executions I expect that is true.'

'Painless, she said.'

'I doubt that.'

'You needed a good axe-man, but a really important prisoner could ask for the man he wanted. Or she could, I suppose HM was thinking of Mary Stuart.'

Later, she said: 'It would be wrong to say that the Queen solved the case, but she put me on the right track. She said thoughtfully: "Of course, there is usually a good practical reason for an execution."' In the case of her ancestors, Charmian recalled, it had been to get them out of the way. Some people are too dangerous to be allowed to live.

Their conversation was pleasant but short. Charmian provided all the details about the finding of the body and the head which she felt ready to pass on to her sovereign, and found to her amusement that the Queen was well informed. She must have read all the newspapers with thoroughness. Of course, the jump season was over and the flat racing had not really got under way, there was a hiatus, an interesting murder on one's own doorstep filled it in. One was interested but not amused.

'Well, and how was that?' asked Lady Mary, coming up to them where they stood in the window embrasure while Charmian collected herself. 'Ordeal by fire over safely?'

'I think so. Easy really, I just answered questions.'

'Shelled you like a pea, did she? That's the usual style.' She began to move away. 'Forgive me, duties to attend to.' They saw her at her door, giving a neat bob and making royalist noises.

'We can go now,' said Humphrey. 'I booked a table at Holy Joe's and I'm getting hungry.'

Holy Joe's was the Italian restaurant on Church Square which was owned by Joseph Sancta who said he was Italian but whom Humphrey, who always knew these things, said was Maltese. It was a good restaurant where you could trust the wine. Charmian and

103

Humphrey ate there often.

The real name of the restaurant was the Padovani, but no one seemed to accept that Joe had come from Padua, nor did he ever claim it, while Humphrey also said that Sliema was a much more likely birthplace. The Padovani was in a narrow three-storey house with a few tables and a bar on the ground floor, a narrow staircase which led past the kitchens which were sandwiched between ground level and the top floor where were the choicest tables. There was a basement room leading out to a paved garden where you ate in summer. Humphrey and Charmian being favoured patrons were led to a good table by a large window.

'You order ... I want to make a telephone call.'

Charmian took herself off to an alcove on the stairway where she could hear noises from above, below and from the kitchen. In many ways the Padovani was a strangely arranged place but it flourished because the food was good.

Once more she dialled Emily's lodging house. This time the girl herself answered.

'Emily, I don't think you should stay where you are, on your own, I want you to go to some friends of mine. Birdie Peacock and Winifred Eagle, they live in the close just behind Maid of Honour Row, so you will be near me.'

There was silence.

'I don't know if you know them, but they are

104

good friends of mine and nice women, you will like them.'

'I don't know them,' said Emily; she did not sound pleased at the idea. 'Well, I've met them but not to really know.'

'They are very open-minded and liberal in their ideas...' Charmian did not want to go into details about the two, whose lifestyle was indeed hard to describe, but of their goodness of heart and charity she could be sure. Integrity of their own kind, too. 'I think you'll like them. They have all sorts of interests.' An understatement really, but she could go into it more later.

'I have heard about their ways, I think Nancy went to one of their sessions on health and nature when she knew she was ill... Didn't cure her, though.'

'No, they have never claimed to be able to cure illness.' Warts, maybe, but not death, and death is what your family seems richly infected with.

'Thanks for thinking about me.' Emily sounded polite but far from grateful. Her voice was strained, rough, as if she had been crying or shouting. 'But I won't go. Thanks all the same.'

'I don't want you to stay where you are. Once the press find your address, and they will, they will be camping out on your doorstep. It's not safe.'

'I think they are here now, or they have been.

105

I hid in the loo,' said Emily without much interest. 'I don't feel threatened. What danger can I be in?'

'I don't know. It's a feeling I have. There is a killer out there and you know it. You probably know the killer without realizing it. Or putting a name or a face. Do it for me, please, Emily.'

There was silence, before a grudging yes. Goodness, the girl sounded odd.

'Is anyone there?'

'No, of course not.'

I don't know about that, thought Charmian. 'Look after yourself.' But the line was already dead.

*   *   *

'I have ordered,' said Humphrey, 'taking advice from Joe who said the fish is best tonight. Also his new soup to start ... You had better eat, you're getting tired.' He touched her hand.

'No, not tired. But worried. I think that girl Emily might be in danger.'

'Why do you think that?' He was watching her face where he saw strain. She was puzzled, not like his Charmian who usually saw life so clear.

Charmian drank some soup, which was rich and strong. 'I don't know. I just have this feeling of something wrong, and I have learned to trust those feelings when they come.'

'So what have you done?'

'I have sent her to stay with Birdie and Winifred ... I hope I've done the right thing. But time will show.'

Humphrey looked at her, assessing her thoughts. 'They can look after themselves,' he said quietly.

'I think they can.'

'But I wish you hadn't got into this case in such a personal way.'

'I couldn't help it. I am involved in a personal way. Margaret Drue seems to have sent me a plea for help. She must have known she was going to be killed and tried to get a message to me.'

'Tried? What does that mean?'

'I'm guessing that she was imprisoned somewhere before being killed. I didn't know her but a number of people who knew me also knew her.' The hairdresser, Beryl Barker, and the two witches. 'And they may not have been the only ones, I leave out the Queen and Lady Mary but there could have been others. I was getting a lot of publicity about then, name and face in the papers. A scrap of paper with my name and face may have been all she had by way of a message.' It was an unpleasing picture and not one she cared for.

She could talk freely to her husband, and she usually did so. He complained that she kept things to herself too much, but the truth was that she talked more freely to him than to

107

anyone outside her professional team.

'It's a very terrible case and still building up. Dolly has come back with hints of child abuse, and Rewley,' she paused to think about Rewley, and sighed, 'He is delivering an informant, sex unknown, who is talking of more human remains...'

Her husband poured her some more wine. 'Come on, cheer up. You've had worse cases. Just keep out of danger yourself, will you please?'

'Oh, I'm in no danger.'

'You've said that before...'

Charmian shrugged. 'It's only what comes with the job ... And don't say, but now my job is being your wife, or you will be the one in danger.'

'I wouldn't dream of it.'

'I know it, forgive me.' She bent forward and put her hand on her husband's. 'Let's talk about the house and where we are going to live. How would you feel about staying in Maid of Honour Row? I have to admit I am fond of it.' And it suited the cat, although better not mention that.

'I like it too. Not everyone can claim to have witches for neighbours.'

The waiter approached. 'Madam, the instrument in your coat pocket...'

Charmian rose to her feet. 'Oh God, my bleeper. Sorry everyone. Why did I bring it?'

Why indeed, thought her husband, watching

her go to the telephone. Because you are you, that's why.

She was some time coming back.

'It was Dolly ... she's picked up some news. The body in the basement is not that of Margaret Drue. It's an unknown woman...'

Humphrey looked at her silently.

'And that is not the worst of it ... Emily is missing.'

'But you've only just spoken to her.'

'She has not gone round to Winnie and Birdie ... All right, perhaps there hasn't been much time ... But the door of her room was open, no sign of her in the room, and there is blood all over it.'

CHAPTER FIVE

'What does it mean?' He was asking the question to slow her down; he thought she was driving far too fast.

'It means that Margaret Drue might be still alive and has attacked Emily.'

'That's jumping to a conclusion. Two conclusions: one about Drue and one about Emily.'

'I'm thinking aloud. You needn't listen. Anyway, you asked the question.'

That was true. 'Where are we going?' he said, looking out to the car window. He knew she shouldn't have been the one to drive: this was not the way back to Maid of Honour Row. Home might be where the heart is, as his dear love had said earlier this evening, but it did not seem to be the place where she often rested.

'To Emily's lodgings, of course.'

'Do you hear that noise? It's me groaning.'

Dolly Barstow was standing outside the lodging house; she was deep in talk with a tall, fair-haired young man in jeans and a sweatshirt, student uniform, but she was keeping an eye out all the same, and saw Charmian at once.

'I thought you would still be around. What made you come here?'

'Just curious, and a mite worried about the girl. Hello, Humphrey. Dragged you along too, has she?'

'I am a willing victim.'

Dolly was already leading the way in. 'It's a mess in there, you won't like what you see.'

'It was a mess before. I suspect it's always a mess.'

Charmian was right behind Dolly. Into the room on the right, the door unlocked. Behind them, Humphrey moved more slowly, not sure if he ought to be here or not. This was local police business and probably even his wife and Dolly were pushing it a bit, SRADIC being something else again.

The same thought occurred to Charmian, who looked to observe at least the appearance of the rules; she didn't want to get across Superintendent Horris more than she need. He was famous for his iron moods. It must be time for one to descend upon him; he was no lover of women in the force, women in authority, which he was inclined to equate with women interfering.

'Whom have you told about Emily?'

The answer she expected came at once. 'Jim Towers. He's coming round. He may have told HG, depends how important he thinks it.'

Charmian took a deep breath, and ran through the categories of those whose absence required investigation. 'Well, Emily is not under the age of sixteen, she is not mentally or physically impaired. Nor is she a senile old lady. Nor has she been gone long. On the other hand she has been touched by a murder and you say there is blood, which puts her in the class of involuntary disappearance. I would call that more than interesting at least ... And about the identity, or non-identity of the body?'

'He told me. HG is screaming.' Superintendent Horris had famous rages but his screams were silent, audible only through the grinding of his teeth the better to bite you with. It gave Charmian some pleasure to think of the redoubtable Superintendent wearing his teeth down. 'He had a holiday fixed for the end of next week, and he thought he'd be able to tidy the body in the basement up neatly, and

111

get off. He fishes, you know.'

'What a shame,' said Charmian falsely, then with more truth: 'Good luck for the fish.'

She paused on the threshold of Emily's room; the handsome young man had somehow got in front, was standing in the doorway, listening to all that they were saying.

'Thanks,' Charmian said. 'You've been very helpful.' She took it from Dolly's friendly manner to him that he had been. 'I spoke to you on the telephone earlier, didn't I? Right, we can manage now.'

'It is my house,' he said, not with reproach but with the emphasis of one who was not going to be overlooked.

'You won't go away then. Talk to you later.'

'Emily was a friend.'

'Then I shall certainly want to know all you know about her disappearance. If that is what it is. She may be back any minute.'

'I don't think so,' he said, swinging away. 'You take a look at the room.' Over his shoulder he said: 'Just to get in first, in case you had any dark thoughts about me, I don't beat women up and I was out with friends, and she was here when I left.'

Emily's room had been untidy when Charmian had seen it earlier, but there were signs of upheaval. Drawers were open and their contents thrown around, her cupboard door was open with the clothes tumbled on to the floor, not that she had many. 'Not a dressy girl, our Emily.'

'Unless she's taken them with her.'

Charmian surveyed the room. 'You think this is just a sign of hasty packing? You could be right ... What about the blood? Where is it, by the way?'

Dolly pointed to the wash basin hidden behind a half-drawn curtain. 'There ... and she didn't just do that shaving.'

A pool of blood was congealing at the bottom of the basin where the waste pipe was plugged with a sponge soaked in blood. Red splashed the sides of the basin, the looking-glass above and the wall around.

'Wonder what blood group she is,' said Charmian thoughtfully. 'I suppose it is human blood? Well, we shall find out.'

'You don't sound very sympathetic.'

'I'm irritated with her. I knew something was going to happen and I tried to get her away. She was difficult about it.'

Humphrey had been wandering round the room, looking at the confusion of books and papers on the floor but carefully not touching anything.

Emily had her work desk in the window where the light was better; this too was in some disorder but it may have been how she kept it because the notebook was open and the pen laid across it as if she had just put it down. Various photographs, one of Emily, a younger Emily, with a dog; one of an older woman whom he took to be her sister Nancy. Some holiday snaps, children on a beach, and on the wall to the right of the desk, a photograph of an elderly man. Her father? Next to this was a large group photograph. Two rows of youngsters, sitting neatly, legs together, hands folded on the lap. Girls in neat starched dresses and boys in linen tunics over short trousers.

'Those were the days, reminds me of my pre-prepper.'

Around the children stood the teaching staff, two women beside Nancy and a youngish man. It had not been a large school. In the background there were several other women who might be teachers or part of the domestic staff, a healthy looking man, feet akimbo, who was perhaps the gardener, and another, more delicate looking.

'Art or music?' Humphrey wondered aloud.

He didn't touch the photograph, but he went close. 'What's this?'

The two women came over. 'That's a rhetorical question, I take it? A school group. I'm surprised she had it because she showed no signs of liking the school and she was not a pupil there herself.'

'She's in the picture, though.' Dolly was looking over her shoulder. 'There she is, that tall streak with long plaits next to Nancy. And that's their father, the grumpy chap in tweeds standing at the back ... I suppose that's why she has it. Family portrait, maybe the only one

114

she has.' Wrapping a tissue round her fingers to protect the frame, she picked it up. 'Don't know any of the others, though. Margaret Drue must be among the teachers . . . Wonder if one of the kids is Alana?'

She turned over the picture. A sheet of paper was pasted on the back with names written on it, roughly aligned with the adult figures.

'I was right: that's papa, that's Nancy . . . there's Margaret Drue. The woman next to her is Madelaine Mason, not a name I know. That's Maisie Nisbett, she's still around, works in the police canteen, nice woman . . . oh look, that's Dr Yeldon, retired now but you still see him at everything, he must have been the school doctor . . . Harry Fraser, Archie Rose, don't know them.'

Jim Towers walked into the room while Dolly was still intent on the picture which she had now turned over to look at again. 'Who is this chubby fellow, sitting there so neat in a dark suit with his hair cut short?'

She held it out to Charmian who gave it a quick look, then smiled. 'If you don't know, then you'd better guess.'

Jim Towers had seen it. 'Oh you've got that photograph. Got one myself. I must see where it is, haven't seen it for yonks . . . Yes, that was me. I was the school's Friendly Policeman. It was a new trick then; I used to go in every so often and talk to them about crossing the road safely and not talking to strangers.'

115

'Take a look at that photograph, will you? Is Alana one of those children?'

He did not answer.

'She must be, mustn't she?'

He seemed to gather himself, settling himself in his skin. 'Yes, let's have a look. I won't touch it, Dolly, you hold it up ... Mind you, I might not know her face.'

Oh I think you will, Charmian watched him. He did not take overlong as his eyes moved down the rows.

'I think this is her. Pretty sure.' A small delicately featured face with a crest of curly hair.

'Sitting next to you?'

'That's right. It's how I remember her.'

'Pretty little creature,' said Charmian sadly.

Jim Towers looked into the past. 'No, no she wasn't really, not pretty, but she had expression and liveliness ... She might have been beautiful one day.'

Humphrey, who was looking out of the window, said: 'Two police cars drawing up, and one black car.' The cavalry had arrived.

H. G. Horris had come with a formidable show. He was not pleased to see Charmian already there, together with Dolly Barstow, whom he called her acolyte, and his own Inspector Towers, all, as he said to himself, bloody hobnobbing. There was also present a man whom he did not know, although he guessed he could put a name to him. But he

116

decided to be halfway polite.

'Evening, ma'am.' He ignored Dolly and the stranger. 'See you got here, Jim.'

Towers nodded. 'Just arrived.'

'Ah...' The Superintendent looked at Charmian.

'I was here earlier, looked in on my way home.' She did not mention Dolly, but he probably guessed that Dolly had told her and that Dolly had passed the news on to Jim Towers. 'Don't want to interfere but I am worried about the girl.'

'Don't like a girl who has just turned up a dead body in her old home to go missing myself. And certainly not in a welter of blood ... Where is the blood, by the way?'

He was moving round the room. 'Messy young woman by the look of her, doesn't keep the place sparkling clean. Nor tidy ... Ah, there's the blood, we don't know it's hers yet.'

He finished his perambulation of the room. 'It's a nasty sight and not what I'd want to come home to, but we don't know that the girl is missing, do we? In fact, she isn't, not yet. She has hardly been gone for more than an hour or two as far as I can make out. I can't say I like it, but it seems a bit early to start crying murder.' He turned to Charmian. 'Now my idea is that we have a word with that young man who is sitting on the stairs, tell him to look out for her and let us know at once if she comes home, and that we lock the door ... I take it it does lock?

117

... and go home ourselves. We can see in the morning. What do you think?'

Charmian looked at Dolly Barstow, and Dolly responded. 'I'd like to stay on a while, and see.'

'I agree to talking to the landlord,' said Charmian. 'What's his name, by the way?'

'Arnold. Trevor Arnold.' Dolly had got all the facts together. She had an idea she was protecting Jim Towers, although from what, she was not clear. Without meaning to, she gave him a smile, but he did not smile back. Turning to catch Superintendent Horris's interested eyes, she thought that wise.

'Let's get Arnold in then,' said Horris. And to Charmian: 'You taking an interest in this, ma'am?'

'Personally, yes, I'm bound to, since I was there with the girl when the body and head were found, and my name was on the body, but professionally...' she shrugged. 'That very encounter complicates it. I think I shall take advice.'

'As far as I am concerned, ma'am,' he threw his arms out wide, 'you can sit in on everything.'

'Thank you.'

'You will have heard that the body is not that of Drue? Teeth and blood group all wrong. Drue fortunately was well documented. So now we have to find out who we have got.'

'There are some names on the back of that photograph,' said Charmian, pointing.

Towers handed the photograph, still with the piece of tissue that Dolly had used, to the Superintendent, but without supplying the information that he was there in the picture himself.

'You connect her with the school, do you?' said HG absently, as he first looked at the photograph, then turned it over.

'You have to, she is connected, she is in the house.'

'There is that connection certainly.' He was probably grinding his teeth this very minute.

'And the head,' pointed out Charmian. 'The child's head was virtually in her lap.'

He nodded. 'I wasn't forgetting. It is Alana, that's a definite identification, teeth and blood group again.' He was reading the names, then flicking back to the photograph. 'Drue, so that's what she looks like. Eleanor Fraser, I know her, not changed a lot, Madelaine Mason, can't place her face. Maisie Nisbett, only a youngster then, she will have changed.' He looked up and smiled, revealing a quality of charm that did not often appear. 'I get what you are saying: the dead woman might be one of these. Not likely but it gives us a start. You and I both know what you need is a start. Get a name, check it, it's wrong, but it gives you an idea, you can move on from there. Identification, motive, means, opportunity.'

119

He gave Charmian a wry look. 'It seems it's not clear how long that body had been a body, when she was killed. I've asked for an answer quick.'

'Yes, it's important. But the newspaper cutting gives some indication, doesn't it?'

'Well, there again, it may not. You didn't have a chance to handle it, but it was not dead off the press and had been folded, and kept folded. There are traces on it that forensics are working on.'

'Thanks for telling me.'

'You'd like to be kept informed? Of course, I know you have channels...' he carefully did not name them, but she knew whom he meant.

'Just ask Inspector Towers to keep me posted,' she said smoothly.

'Ah yes, Jim,' he looked towards the door where Towers and Arnold had not yet appeared. 'He's taking his time ... I may have to let Jim have a bit of leave.'

'Oh?'

'He's involved too, you see ... That was his face in the photograph, wasn't it?' He could frame a question like an accusation. 'Living portrait.'

Across the room, Humphrey was sitting talking to Dolly who was watching the door for Jim Towers.

Arnold was in the room first, with Towers behind. 'I went up to have a shower. I didn't know you wanted me. When I did want to talk

120

to you, I got pushed out.' He gave Charmian a reproachful look. 'I'm not Emily's keeper, just her landlord. She pays her rent, I'm happy.'

'You a student too, Mr Arnold?' HG was bland.

'I'm doing a PhD and I also have a junior lectureship.'

'You didn't hear or see anything to explain why Emily might have gone off?'

'No. She was here earlier, because I saw her and spoke to her. She doesn't go out a lot in the evening, but she's free, she does what she likes, nothing to do with me.'

'Still, she doesn't often stay out all night?'

'She might do, I don't check. I don't think so though, if you want me to say. But I don't know where she has gone now, she could be back any minute and not thanking us.'

'No idea either about the blood? You didn't hear anything? Noise, shouting, anything?'

'No, I was out at first, then playing music, so I wouldn't hear a noise unless it was very loud. I live on the top floor and I was having a Wagner evening, you don't hear much above *The Ring*.'

'Anyone else in the house?'

'I have one other lodger, but he's away.' Arnold hesitated, then said: 'Emily's been in a very dodgy state, moodwise. Worried about her house. She didn't want to sell it, but she was getting pressure on that. She had some hang-up about the house, she said it ought to be left empty and drop to bits . . . I suppose that might happen now.'

Horris looked in question at Charmian, who shrugged.

'Thank you then, Mr Arnold, we'll leave it there. I'll tell you what we are going to do: we are going to lock up this room and come back tomorrow and you are going to tell us if Emily comes back in the night.'

'You mean I'll have to stay awake all night?'

'I think she will wake you if she wants to get in,' said Horris drily. 'Right?'

'You don't think she will come back?'

'Perhaps not tonight. I am keeping an open mind. You do the same.'

They left the room as it was. The door was locked, and Horris pocketed the key. 'He'll have another one, landlords always do.' He gave Humphrey a smile which said I know who you are and you know who I am, no introduction needed, and you agree with me about landlords, eh?

At the door, Charmian found herself near Jim Towers and not near the other three, so on the pavement outside she said in a low voice: 'I find it strange when you liked the child Alana so much that you lost that photograph.'

He hesitated, then said: 'I think my wife burnt it.'

He moved away then, to speak to the Superintendent, while Charmian considered what she had heard. In a way, it confirmed

122

what she had thought, that Jim Towers was a complicated man caught up in a complex matter.

Dolly came up to say goodbye. 'So it goes, eh?'

And what does that mean, Charmian asked herself. 'We will talk tomorrow. And try to find out what Rewley is up to.'

'Will do,' and Dolly walked over to where Jim Towers was getting into his car.

HG had finished with Towers and left him to Dolly. 'I'll see you get all you want, ma'am.' He gave Charmian something between a bow and a salute, but he had a knowing air. I'll show you, it said. Then he nodded to her husband. 'Goodbye, Sir Humphrey.'

As they drove away, Humphrey said quietly: 'Was that policeman Horris being offensive to you?'

'No. He was only protecting his territory.'

Lions did it, cats did it, and so did policemen. She had done it herself when necessary. It went with the job.

CHAPTER SIX

Dolly Barstow and Jim Towers drove away from the lodging house where Emily's blood, if indeed it was her blood, still lay untouched awaiting forensic tests tomorrow. They drove

123

in separate cars but arrived together outside Dolly's house. It seemed better that way.

'Have you told HG?' she asked.

'Told him that my wife has thrown me out? No, and I shan't until I have to.'

'He's bound to find out.'

'Which is why I won't bother telling him.'

They were standing outside the house while Dolly locked her car and looked for the house keys.

'Come and have a drink.' She looked at his face, drawn and tired, with a kind of quiet misery behind it. I don't make this man happy, she told herself, but perhaps no one could. She went on trying though and the sex was good. 'You don't have to go, you know.'

He nodded, 'I know, my love, but I will. It's better.'

Towers had moved himself into a one-room flat on the road to Cheasey; it was not elegant but it was clean, reasonably comfortable and cheap. He still had a wife and two children to support, together with the mortgage on the family home, there was not much left.

Dolly too had moved recently. After Kate died, she found she could no longer bear the flat they had once shared. So she had found a small house on the edge of the Great Park; it was a longer drive to work but she knew none of the neighbours and none of them knew her. It seemed a time for anonymity.

They walked into the small hall which was

still crowded with tea-chests of her possessions so far unpacked. Two months had passed since moving day, and they were still there. Sometimes Dolly thought she might move away again without the chests ever having been emptied.

'Come into the kitchen while I make some coffee. And give yourself a drink ... there's whisky over there. Should be some clean glasses.'

The kitchen was fitted with a dishwasher which Dolly had never opened. Every morning she rinsed out one cup and saucer and one plate, and left them to drain. All the other meals were taken in the police canteen.

A small laundry abutted on the kitchen with all automatic equipment in the way of washing and drying. Dolly threw in her dirty clothes as they came off and when she had run out of clean ones, then she switched on the washing programme. Once or twice she had been obliged to go out and buy new supplies of pants and bras when even this small chore had been passed by.

I'm getting to be a slut, she told herself. Tidy though, a tidy slut.

'Will you have a drink?' Jim was pouring himself a drink.

'I'll have coffee. Do you want some as well?'

She poured him a cup anyway, noting with relief that he was not taking a big draught of whisky. If he wasn't going to stay, she didn't

125

want him driving home with a heavy whisky load on an empty stomach. Trouble could follow there. If she had had any food in the house except for a grapefruit and an aged lemon, she would have fed him. Not even cat food, there being no cat.

How unlike Charmian, successful, married, happy, and a cat owner ... I was on the way to all that ... she looked at the kettle while it heated, seeing her distorted image in it ... but I seem to have lost the knack. Where am I going now?

He took the coffee without a comment and drank it down apparently without noticing, leaning against the sink unit.

'I was surprised to see you in that photograph. I'd have known you, though.' Although she had not, at first.

'Sometimes it seems a long while ago since that young man sat there in a row and I have thought he was dead, but he is still there inside and he came alive today.'

Dolly put her hand on his: 'You would tell me if I could do anything?'

'That child had to be avenged.'

'I never think revenge is a good thing,' said Dolly.

'I said avenge, not revenge.'

'But they come together, don't they? Hard to tell one from another.' Perhaps one should leave avenging to the gods, she thought. If they are around and interested. Once or twice she had felt that they were, and actively intervening.

He didn't answer directly, but what he said related to the finding of the photograph. 'Daniels, she's a good friend of yours?'

'I don't see so much of her since she married.'

'But you work in her unit SRADIC, she's a power-puller, isn't she? George Rewley, he's with you. He's a high-flyer as well.'

'I don't know if he still is.' We have both been lamed by the same arrow, Kate's death. Or were we both getting to the point beyond which we could not go, and her death just marked the spot?

He finished his whisky, stood up and took a deep, slow breath. 'I'll push off. Thanks for everything. You help me more than you know.'

I know, Dolly thought, what you don't know is what it costs.

She walked to the door with him. 'You know, I think of those people in the photograph, Dr Yeldon, Harry Fraser ... Nancy herself, she's gone now, she came under suspicion. The postie, he's not in the picture, he was under suspicion a bit because he talked to the children, dead now. Maisie Nisbett, the Baileys, the rest ... they make a kind of circle and hang around.'

Dolly stood there with the door open; he was halfway through before he turned round. 'I've changed my mind. Can I stay?'

127

'Of course you can . . . Come on.' She put her arm round him and led him back inside the house, giving him a hug of sympathy . . . Charmian, she apotheosized with a sigh, in case you are thinking of me, which you probably are not, this is not a night of love.

*   *   *

As it happened there was a street party that night of the circle which Dolly had named, the friends of Alana, or as much of it as remained. At that time Dr Yeldon and others did not know that Emily was missing.

The party was not in the street because of the inclement weather but it was held in Dr Yeldon's sitting room, a large room with a conservatory off it. He was a good gardener but age and increasing infirmity had pushed him to gardening indoors, hence the greenhouse.

A street party was Dr Yeldon's name for it, he was old and allowed that sort of joke, but it was more truly a group of people who had lived through the first horror and now felt a need to meet and talk about it. The first gathering of these people had been called a street party because several of those who came to it had lived in River Street, where Dr Yeldon still lived, or close by. But all of them had either worked at Bailey's School or had some connection with it.

128

'We were more in number then,' said Dr Yeldon, looking around the room while his wife poured coffee for them. Mugs. She had moved with the times and knew that mugs were the thing. He picked up a sheet of writing, yellowing somewhat with age, from his desk and studied it. 'Some are dead, and others have moved away.'

He put on thin, wire-framed spectacles which had now, as his granddaughter told him, become chic again, to run through the list.

'Archie Rose and his daughter,' he looked towards them with a smile. 'Both here today . . . How's the arthritis, Archie? And Fanny, don't get too thin, will you?' Fanny was a photographic model but it was her hair and hands that got photographed, you never saw her face or body, but Fanny liked to keep trim, just as her father still gardened. 'Harry Fraser . . . here you are, Harry, just as you were that day, and Eleanor too.'

'We liked the child,' said Eleanor, who usually spoke for them both. 'A great little dancer.'

Dr Yeldon went on: 'Then there was that dear old chap the postman, not with us any longer . . . I never understood why he got suspected.'

'Because he talked to Alana,' said Mrs Yeldon, in her firm, crisp voice. 'Dangerous child.'

'He talked to them all. It's a sad world where

if you are kind to a child, you are suspected of abuse and worse.'

'It is a sad world,' said Mrs Yeldon. 'But he's out of it now.'

'And then there was the young policeman ... he came to talk to us that day.'

'Just looked in,' said his wife.

'Just looked in, yes. But it was good of him to come. He was moved, one could see that.' He adjusted his spectacles, which his wife claimed he used as his worry object. 'I don't think we saw him again, although I may forget, I know I am forgetful, but I understand he has had several promotions. I saw his name mentioned in connection with the recent dreadful discoveries.'

'Towers,' said his wife. 'Inspector Towers.'

'SO HE IS STILL AROUND.' Billy Yeldon managed to make it sound like capital letters. His wife looked alarmed.

'I never liked him,' said Eleanor Fraser, suddenly and unasked. 'Too intense.' Nor was she a great admirer of Mrs Yeldon. Both having been dancers, there was some rivalry. Maud Yeldon had accused Eleanor of not conducting herself properly while in class and Eleanor had replied with counter-accusations of her own.

'Now, Nelly,' began Mrs Yeldon. 'I shall have to remind you ...'

'You keep your secrets, Maud, and I will keep mine.'

130

Another woman came into the room. 'Sorry I am late.' Maisie Nisbett, now married and Mrs Halliday, was thin and eager. 'I just couldn't seem to get cleared up today and you can't go out leaving dirty dishes. Auntie is coming, she's slower than ever this evening, but she's just behind.'

Mrs Nisbett propelled herself through the door, not so much slow as large, Eleanor Fraser thought.

Behind her came a cluster of others of the 'street party', neighbours who lived in this part of Windsor, between the Castle and river, and who had come to the original street party out of interest and compassion. Mrs Alice Otter, widow, Brian Underwood and his wife Mattie, Dr Englehart and his girlfriend Susie. The last two had not been part of the first meeting but had been asked because Dr Englehart taught sociology at the local university and Susie was a lawyer.

Mrs Yeldon had finished handing round the coffee; she was beginning to mutter advice to her husband in a quiet voice: 'Get on with it, Billy.' She sounded angry.

Dr Yeldon considered whether they should open with a prayer but on looking at the people assembled there, he decided that they were a pretty secular roomful and better, as his wife was suggesting, just to get on with it. He liked to take her advice because she was a powerful woman.

131

'Here we go then, you know why we are here.' He braced his shoulders for the attack; it felt like going over the top as he looked at his audience, eyes wide, expecting something good from him, except for Dr Englehart who looked sceptical and Susie who looked neutral. 'Last time, when Alana died in such a horrible way, we met to pledge ourselves to help find her killer. Then it looked as though the teacher, Margaret Drue, had killed her and fled. We said we would look for her. I know that we did, several items came from you of possible sightings. But gradually they tailed away and I realized, you realized, that we were not going to find her.' He paused to see if he had their attention. 'But now she has been discovered, dead. With a child's head on her lap. How did this happen, I ask myself. Is it a revenge killing?'

'We don't know that it's Margaret Drue,' said Dr Englehart.

'But we think so.'

'Only guessing it's Margaret Drue. Don't really know. It may not be.' He added: 'In fact, there's a rumour going round that it isn't her.'

Dr Yeldon appeared discomfited, he was not used to being questioned, but he was an honest man. 'Well, I'll just have to start thinking about that.'

The door opened for Eddy Bell. 'Come in, Eddy. Glad you could make it . . .' He looked round the room. 'Eddy didn't attend our

132

session last time...'

'I was still at school,' said Eddy.

'But this time, taking the circumstances into account, it seems right he should be.'

'Couldn't get Big Albert. Once he's finished for the day, he likes to get off on his own.'

'And Emily?'

'Haven't seen her. Honest, I never really tried, Doc. We're not that close. She employed me but that's about it.'

The door opened again for Winifred Eagle to come in.

'Winnie—how did you know?'

'I have my channels,' she said with dignity. In fact, Mrs Yeldon had told her, but why say so? ('Come and stop my old boy making a fool of himself,' she had said, 'he can't do anything, we can't do anything, couldn't before, but he says it is a necessary human gesture.') 'Birdie can't be with us, we have been expecting a visitor who has not turned up.' Emily, in fact. 'She remains at home, in case.'

'Stop talking like the Queen,' said Billy Yeldon irritably, 'and be normal. You're welcome if you behave.'

With dignity, Winnie said: 'I always behave.'

'And remember I am Church of England. No witch work.' The two had crossed on this issue before. As a man of science and a church warden at St Mary's, the doctor would have no necromancy.

Over the coffee mugs the discussion went on,

133

but nothing, to Dr Yeldon's disappointment and to his wife's total unsurprise, of interest came out. With sympathy, she saw him pucker his lips. Poor old boy, he did try to get a result, he watched too much TV detection, life was not like that. She knew the difference between fantasy and reality, as he had done once, but he dreamed too much now.

He was taping all that went on in this room, she knew it, but she wondered if the rest of the party knew it. Wasted tape, she thought, still it doesn't cost much. Poor old boy, she mustn't be bad to him. He was one of those she would protect.

Nevertheless, as was later understood, something important was said at the evening, on which, as it ended, someone laughed.

As they broke up, they gossiped. And there was a laugh.

'Saw you talking to Emily,' said Eleanor Fraser to Eddy. There was iron in her voice.

'Oh come on, Nelly,' said Maud Yeldon with irritation. 'What does it matter.' Don't gossip, she meant.

'Didn't I, Eddy?' persisted Mrs Fraser.

Eddy shuffled his feet. 'Oh well, yeah, we talk.'

'Over coffee in the Coffee Pot in Ship Street?'

'Oh well, just a cup, old schoolmates after all, but we aren't out of...'

'The same social class?' said Winifred Eagle.

'Yeah, something like that.' Eddy shifted in his chair.

'She looked upset,' said Eleanor.

'Nelly!' reproved Maud Yeldon.

Eddy got up to go. 'I dunno about that. Course, we found that body and the head, that wasn't good news.'

'Come on, Eddy, you're a poor liar. What was it?'

Eddy looked as if he would like to have claimed he was a very good liar, but thought better of it. 'She thought someone was after her,' he said grudgingly, but truthfully. This had been it. 'I mean that's what she said.'

'Who?' asked Dr Yeldon.

Eddy was silent for a moment. 'Didn't say. I think it was a woman.'

There was an instant of silence, everyone had heard. Eleanor Fraser looked surprised, and not best pleased, at what she had got; Mrs Yeldon shook her head and looked grave. Winnie Eagle said nothing, but the dark thoughts she had already been nourishing about Emily's non-appearance were reinforced.

'We have to tell the police.'

'I came past where she lives,' said Dr Englehart's Susie, who had taken more interest than she had previously owned to; she had come this evening on purpose to listen to this group. 'And I saw signs of police activity.'

Dr Yeldon stood up, his face eager. 'We

135

must go to them. At once.'

His wife took him in hand. 'No, Billy.' She was firm. 'They clearly know what there is to know already. The police are there. You just heard.'

'I am glad I have the tape of our meeting. It is testimony, is it not?' he said, in a tired way.

'You let the police get on with it.' And much good might they do, she had little respect for them. Superintendent H. G. Horris, and the doubtful young policeman, now Inspector Towers, she had taken pains to learn their names. She was worried though, it didn't sound good. She did not like the idea of the police fussing round.

But she did not say this aloud, putting all her skill and tact into speeding her guests on their way. When all the party had left, she urged her husband to bed and to sleep; she was worried by his anxious face. You got strokes looking like that. It was in her mind to destroy that tape of the meeting. She didn't like it. Billy was too innocent for his own good and did not understand the dangers of what he did. 'Let me have that tape, dear, and stop worrying and go to sleep.'

'I can't go to sleep now.'

'Don't worry. The police won't go to sleep.' She smiled, but they could be blinded.

*   *   *

136

Jim Towers was asleep, but dreaming badly. Heads were rolling all around him, eyes open, tongues wagging.

H. G. Horris was asleep; he was not dreaming because on a pad by his bed he had made notes of his thoughts, and followed this by mapping out his morrow.

The investigating team was already in place, dealing with the dead body; in spite of the interference (in private he used a coarser word) of SRADIC, or possibly with the help of it, the identity of the woman would be established.

Then they would find out how she came to have the child's head. How and when she died would emerge, and possibly from that he would evolve where. And by whose hand. Not from suicide, the medical evidence made that clear, even if he had thought so for a moment.

The head and its condition puzzled him, but an answer would come. No fear there, they could be brilliant the scientists. He did not depend on them, but by God, they could be useful.

The body of the woman was now with the pathologists, the forensic boys were hovering too. The mortuary was her home at present, and would be for some weeks. But there would be an inquest; even if it would have to be adjourned, he was prepared.

Tomorrow morning, as his notes told him, he would visit the Incident Room, speaking with several of the officers; each day he would choose different ones, in what he hoped was a spontaneous manner but which his subordinates accurately assessed as being on a plan, not alphabetical, they thought. So possibly by age. Or even by the colour of the eyes.

Then he would go back to the office where he would read all reports, faxes and print-outs. Then he would summon Jim Towers and suggest he took some leave, he had plenty due to him. Or he could call in sick.

The bloody room and the absence of Emily, if she was still not there, was a problem he would deal with as need arose. Before he went to bed, he sent a message to the Incident Room telling them to send a team round there in the morning and be ready for him.

Confident in his professional life, convinced that he would outlast the brash newcomer SRADIC, secure in his private life (although unsuspected by him, this was about to burst out), Horris slept peacefully. His private life, which he kept private, he conducted with more licence than was guessed at.

*　　　*　　　*

George Rewley was not asleep, not even in bed, not even thinking about bed, he was walking the streets of Windsor, which he had done many a night since the death of Kate.

Windsor, as well as being a royal town, was a

quiet, respectable one; if anything violent took place in the streets like vandalism or any affray, it was usual to say: 'Oh they came from Cheasey'—that outpost of villainy, or Slough, or Hounslow, or even London. There were rough customers about Windsor at night, but there was something about Rewley's figure, walking, walking, which repelled any idea of attack even from those high on drink or drugs who might have thought of it.

However, on this night, the night when Emily's room had been emptied and bloodstained, he was walking with a practical reason: he was looking for his informer, who had let him down.

Charmian had deliberately set him to check a series of mundane, boring cases of corruption in a certain local office. She had no intention of involving him in the Flanders Road affair because of the child. No one could stop him thinking about it, though. He had not been in Windsor at the time of the original murder of Alana. If he had been, and if Charmian Daniels had been there, then he thought they would have made a better job of it. He had got out the case records from the original report, read through all the statements, all the questioning of witnesses, all the forensic and medical evidence, and come to the conclusion it was a botched job.

He couldn't explain why: everything had been done according to the rules, all done as it should be done, no looseness exactly, but a complete lack of imagination, as if no one mind had ever got to work on the case. It was a team effort which did not come to life.

He had taken it slowly, over a period of days; he did not neglect his other work, boring as it was. Chosen to be so, he knew Charmian well enough to work that out. He also suspected that one of the reasons the files he needed on the child's death were not always available to him was because she was studying them. It would be in character, it was what she would do.

At the end of one day's work, Rewley had closed the files, and gone to drink coffee in the canteen. Two nights ago now.

So that was how it was, he thought. The police team seemed obsessed with Margaret Drue on account of her record. It had to be her. Several of them had known her briefly, or seen her around the town and not liked her. Probably she was not likeable, although the evidence of Nancy Bailey was that she was a good and efficient teacher.

Rewley noted that her abuse of children earlier had always been of young boys, she had never touched a really young child like Alana. And in any case, had undergone therapy and claimed to have changed.

The case was never closed because Margaret Drue disappeared. Her past life was documented, but she herself was gone. Then it had looked as though she had turned up, dead, together, horrible as it was, with the head of the dead child. As soon as he had heard this story, he knew there was something wrong with it. He had a way of picking stories out of the air, and it was no surprise to him when he got the hint that the female body was not that of Margaret Drue.

On that night, two nights ago, the canteen was not crowded but one officer he knew slightly, Jim Towers, was drinking orange juice at the next table. For a moment, they ignored each other, then Rewley moved over to sit at the same table as Towers. 'All right?'

'Fine. I've had too much of my own company.' He knew he was getting too fond of Dolly Barstow, and taking too much from her; he was trying to keep away, he had nothing to give her and she deserved so much more.

He knew George Rewley was a friend of Dolly and a fellow worker in SRADIC, he also knew Rewley had lost his wife. That makes two of us, he had thought, as he saw Rewley across the room. Perhaps it was that very thought that had drawn Rewley to him. No, must be psychic.

'I've been seeing a bit of your boss lately,' he said. 'She was there when the body and the head were found in Flanders Street.'

'I had heard.'

'And her name came up too. One of those coincidences.' Towers gave a half smile.

141

'Threw her a bit, I think, but she's a resilient lady.'

Rewley thought he knew that too. He was taking a profound interest in the case because he had been confronted with a stranger who wanted to tell him what he knew. He had been sitting by himself in the park by the river, something he did a lot lately, not exactly brooding but something very close to it; it was dusk, not much light where he was, when the man came up to him. Even if it had been broad daylight, he could not have seen much of him because he was wearing one of those baseball-type caps with the visor right down over his face, on which dark spectacles rested. His body was clothed in a loose black raincoat like a plastic sack.

'Sir?'

Rewley had looked up. All right, he thought, you don't want to be recognized.

'I want to talk ... I know what you are ...'

'What's it about?'

The figure, man he had to be, kept his voice low. 'It's about a body.' Then he stopped, and looked around nervously. A bunch of teenagers had just surged into the park so that the surveillance lights came on. A car passed on the road. This was, after all, a public park, green and leafy but not private. 'I might need something for it.'

'Money, you mean?'

'Might do.'

142

'I'll have to get permission for that. And I will need a good reason.'

He got no answer; the figure slid away.

That was their first contact. He said nothing about it to anyone, there was nothing to say.

On the next day, he had a telephone call. 'Sir?' This seemed to be the chap's code signal. 'Sir, if you can get me some money I can tell you about some human remains.'

'Oh come on. I want more than that.'

'Flanders Street . . . part of that business.'

Rewley was quiet, but before he could speak, the voice spoke again: 'I'll get in touch. I'll come to the park. I know you go there. Just keep looking for me there.'

Do you? Rewley thought. So you have been watching me? His informer was a local man, he could tell by the accent, in spite of a poor attempt to disguise it by dropping it.

'I'll see you, I'll see you,' said the voice urgently. 'Get me that money.'

This conversation Rewley had reported to Charmian Daniels, and got her cautious approval for the contact. He had not given her all the details of the meeting, which had its horror side, but had sealed them up inside himself to let out later.

He was thinking about this conversation as he sipped his coffee and listened with half an ear to Jim Towers. He knew he was on the point of opening the mental sack in which he had stored the details about his informer.

'We thought we had the identity sewn up,' Towers was saying. 'But now there's a suggestion that it's not Drue after all ... a big surprise all round.'

Rewley was interested now. 'Must be.' There was an odd, ironic note in Towers' voice, as if there was a joke and he knew it.

'Might be a good thing as far as I am concerned,' he was saying. 'Because your boss has been measuring me up for handcuffs.'

'What does that mean?'

Towers laughed. 'Nothing, forget it. Heads you win, tails I lose.' Then he said, 'Perhaps I did get too close in, you shouldn't do that, should you? But somehow I couldn't help it. One thing I will say is that the girl Emily is a mess, and she knows more than she is saying.'

At that point Rewley knew nothing much about Emily except her name. 'What about her?'

'Forget it, sorry I spoke. I lose my head sometimes. Forget that too. I've had heads on my mind ever since the child died years ago.' And it had probably ruined his marriage, this obsession, and might do the same for his career. About his life, he did not think. 'I shouldn't get so close,' said Towers again.

'It happens,' said Rewley. Inside he was saying: we all have obsessions and omissions (although oddly enough this did not make him warm any more to Jim Towers). I didn't tell all the truth to myself about that first meeting with

144

the so called informer ... I sat on it. Now it was coming out.

What did I see? A strange figure, and I don't think I would have been much helped by seeing the face. What I could see was coated in thick white plaster so that the features were smoothed out and all expression eliminated.

I remember leaning towards him—or her— thinking that this was not a funny figure, rather one to haunt the children, and not do much for adults either, something out of a nightmare. Couldn't be a woman, could it? Too thickset. Or was it padding?

As I leaned forward, the figure leaned back, didn't want me to come too close, but I was close enough to notice a strange smell without being able to pin it down. Not a dirty, human smell, as one might have expected, but something else again. Have to think about that, I had thought.

'Why me? Why have you come to me?'

No answer to that one. The strange figure was shaking, the whole figure on the move, head, shoulders, thorax, legs. Only arms and hands, held rigid, were not moving. All informers were odd, never normal, and this one was no exception. All driven by greed, and sometimes hate, and occasionally fear as well, but a shaking one was unusual in Rewley's experience.

Once again, he remembered the smell. It had been a strange scene and viewed in retrospect, now he was letting himself think about it, not a good one. Money for news of more human remains, that seemed to be what was on offer.

What the informer wanted to tell him related to the deaths in the school, but he was not going to say so to Jim Towers. In the first place, this was his informer, and secondly, there was a certain reserve he felt towards the Inspector. No pooling of information here, until Charmian Daniels said so. If ever. She wasn't a lady for sharing.

Towers had finished his drink and stood up. Rewley realized he must have been quiet for some time. What the hell? The two men had parted on polite but not over-friendly terms. Rewley already knew of and did not quite approve of Dolly's relationship with Towers.

All this was in Rewley's mind that night while Towers slept in Dolly Barstow's bed, and H. G. Horris slumbered peacefully, and the circle of Emily's friends also slept, and Rewley walked, hoping to find his informer. He recalled Towers' last remark: 'That girl Emily is a mess, and she knows something she is not telling.'

One more look at the park where no one except a pair of lovers in the bushes and a drunk asleep on the park bench was to be found. The park never closed, the railings were low, and long since broken down here and there. You stepped over them and walked on. He looked in the drunk's face, in case it was his

146

informer, but not so. Then, without conscious thought, he found himself walking towards Emily's lodgings. He knew the address although he had never been there, but the house was in central Windsor and not far for him to walk.

There was one thing about insomnia, he thought, it did give you long working hours. He closed his mind to thoughts of Kate and their child and let his feet do the thinking. They seemed to be thinking about Emily Bailey.

It was late, but not too late, just before midnight, there were lights on in the house. Everyone knew students never went to bed. He rang the doorbell. After a pause it was opened by a tall young man in jeans and sweater but with bare feet. You are not my informer, he said to himself; he was mentally examining everyone he came into contact with and crossing them off the list. You don't smell right. This chap smelt of expensive toilet water.

'Emily Bailey?'

The door seemed to be closing in his face. He put a foot forward.

'Look, who are you?'

Rewley showed his warrant card. He held it out silently.

'Look, Emily is not here. You lot have been here already tonight, you know she's not here and she hasn't left a message since then. No calls, no Emily. Got that?'

'Can I see her room?' Why did he ask that?

He had no real interest in Emily's room but he had prescience.

'It's locked and the big chap took the key. You ask him. I don't know if he thought I would wash away the blood, but he needn't have bothered.'

'Blood?'

'Yes, hers or someone else's, take your pick.'

...That was what I smelt on the informer, blood, hot fresh blood.

'But I'll tell you something for nothing: I think she's gone for good. Dead.'

Rewley stared at the young man. 'Any reason?'

'This came.' He reached behind him and thrust something at Rewley.

'It's a wreath.'

'Right. Ten for observation. You have it. I've already had an old chap here, Dr Yeldon he said, asking to see her. She's not here, I said, and whatever she's got, you can't cure her.'

Rewley looked at it, the white blossoms were faded, the leaves shrunken. 'The flowers are dead.'

'Right again.'

'How long have you had them?'

'I know what you are getting at. They came tonight and they came dead. Work that one out. You have 'em. I don't want them in the house. They are bad luck. Take them to your boss.'

The door closed.

Rewley walked away carrying the flowers like a lost mourner at a long ago funeral feast. They would have to go to Charmian. Then she could do what she thought fit with them. As he walked along, his fingers moved around the surface. There was a card. Beneath a street lamp, he read it: 'With love from Eve, Pete, and family.'

He passed the park once again, from which even the drunk and the lovers seemed to have disappeared. He collected his car to drive home. Some vandal had attacked the door but failed to get in, that was life.

At home, there was a message on his answerphone. That voice, strange yet compelling because it was so full of fear. 'Look: I'm telling you this for free.' A pause, so that Rewley wondered if the caller had gone away, then the voice again.

'I recognized her. I suddenly saw her come out, she popped out of her disguise. There are other remains and might be more. Let me have the money. The price is a hundred pounds and I want it now, I'm scared shitty.

'Six o'clock tomorrow morning in the park. With the money.' The voice was changing all the time, breaking, shifting.

Rewley groaned, suddenly exhausted. He'd be there.

*   *   *

Early in the morning he shaved and drank some coffee, then he drove to the cash machine in the bank opposite the Castle and prayed it would spill out the money he wanted.

CHAPTER SEVEN

'So what happened?' said Charmian. They were in her office, she was sitting at her desk and Rewley was walking about the room, in a way she found worrying but was prepared to put up with because she understood his need to release pent-up energy. She sighed but allowed it, following him with her eyes. I'll be dizzy if he doesn't stop soon, she thought.

'I waited. And I waited. And then I went on waiting.' He took a brisk turn up and down the room; he was tired but he could not rest.

'Sit down and have some coffee while we think it over.' She poured the coffee, looked at his face, and added cream and sugar; her judgement was that Rewley needed all the nourishment he could get. Cholesterol levels need not come into it.

'Let's go over it, what we know and don't know. As of yesterday, we know that Emily has gone, and blood was left in her room.'

'No news about her?'

'Nothing so far; as far as I know she's not back, but it's early. HG will let me know when

150

he knows anything.' He might not be quick about it, but he was too professional (and she was too important) to play about.

'And the woman found in the school with the head in her lap is not Margaret Drue?'

'No, we don't know who she is yet, but it will come out. I don't believe it will be difficult.' She had a candidate in mind and she supposed that HG had also, although the motive for this particular murder was not apparent at the moment. Nor why the body had been left in the cupboard, whenever that had happened, and been gifted with the child's head.

But the old axiom remained: once the identity of the victim had been established, then the motive would become clear. It was interesting about the head, but painful too, it hardly bore thinking about.

'What about the head? No doubt there?' He was drinking his coffee, feeling stronger with every mouthful. It was good to be back working again, good to be with Charmian, she had always been a first-class boss. As well as being Kate's godmother—no, don't go down that avenue. Turn it off.

'Oh yes, no doubt there, it is the child Alana. Her face is recognizable. The puzzle is the condition of the head. It is too good in one way and ghastly in another.'

Rewley sat quiet.

'So that's what we know, and the Investigating Team will have more to tell us, I have no doubt … Now about your informer, he, or she, was frightened?'

'Yes, sex of the informant was a puzzle, the voice was assumed and sounded young with high tones at some times and at others was very deep. So take your pick.'

'What is your pick?'

'I'm thinking about it.'

'But the speaker was frightened?'

'Yes, that was real, I believed in the fear. It came out clearly with that sentence about someone in disguise and the real person "popping out". I think the speaker meant he, I'll call him he, meant that he saw something of this person's true character.'

'Did you get the impression that the person who popped out was a woman or a man?'

Rewley thought about it. 'I ran the tape back several times, it was a bit blurred but I am almost sure that at one point the speaker said "she".'

Charmian drank some more coffee and sat in silence. 'So, are we guessing that this mysterious entity who "popped out"—graphic phrase—is Margaret Drue? I think we can guess so.'

The telephone broke into their conversation. 'Yes, speaking … Morning, HG. What?' She listened. 'Thank you, that is very interesting … Anything about the girl? Well, it is early yet … she may turn up. I would like to come round for a talk … I may have something to add …

Right. See you.'

She turned to Rewley. 'The head of the child was only recently placed with the body; the pathologist says that from all the signs it had been kept in a refrigerator. Frozen, and then' ... she hesitated. 'After that, it may have been boiled.'

'Someone must have a strange home life.'

'You'd think that person would stand out so you could say: Must be him ... or her. But it's not like that, is it, as you and I know. Even the most perverted of murderers can have the most ordinary of faces.'

'It suggests something, though, doesn't it? That the person who kept the head either lives alone, or has somewhere private to keep the head.'

'Or has a willing accomplice.'

'You're not suggesting that the head has been moved from refrigerator to refrigerator over the years?'

'No, I'm not suggesting that, and you mustn't either,' said Charmian sharply. 'I don't like what this case is doing to you. I never wanted you near it.'

'I was dragged into it, pulled, not jumped.' Rewley spoke with force. 'An informer came to me; I didn't even connect what he or she had to say with the Bailey school. And now I think: why to me? I think we will know a lot when we find out the answer to that one.'

'All the same, I'd rather you were out of it.

153

There's a lot of emotion floating around in this case.' More than she could understand, although she was touched by it herself. She had wasted her own time, going around asking questions about Margaret Drue when now it turned out that Drue was not the dead body.

'This may surprise you, but I am not being emotional about this, I am just trying to do my job on a problem that landed on me. I didn't go looking for it, it happened. So on emotion; curiosity, yes, a desire to clear a mystery up, yes, that too, and that's all.'

'I wish I could believe that.' She too had been dragged into it, if it came to that, because her name was actually on the dead body.

'You're mixing me up with Jim Towers.'

'Ah, you've noticed him then?'

'Spoken to him, and yes, a lot of emotion there and the wrong sort ... he's engaged, immersed in the case.'

'He's being taken off the case. HG has noticed it too.' Just give him more time to be with Dolly Barstow, she thought without pleasure. But she trusted Dolly; in the end, Dolly would be sensible.

'What will you do now about your informer?' she asked Rewley.

He shrugged. 'Just wait. Not much else I can do.'

'You will have to tell HG ... not that there's much to tell ...'

'He or she had a kind of seamless face, I

154

suppose that was the mask.' Rewley frowned. 'It wasn't a mask, of course, but something painted on like a clown only more so. Plaster white ... A disconcerting face, I found myself looking away, as you do with a scarred or malformed face ... I wasn't sure what was underneath that face.'

Charmian let him go on without interruption.

'I have a feeling about the person inside that face ... the voice with all its changes might be the clue ... There is a biography in that voice.'

'That's quite a speech you are making,' said Charmian drily. Rewley always had insights, perhaps it would be wiser to let him go, waiting for his informer, trawling in what information he could. H. G. Horris might be grateful.

Rewley looked at her as if she might say something on that point, but she took a sideways step. 'You are not the only one with an informant ... only mine gave a name. Dr Yeldon telephoned to say he wanted to talk to me, to tell me something.'

'He knew the school. He was the school doctor.'

'I know. His name was in the file.'

'I wonder what he wants. I can tell you something, he knows about Emily being missing, he was round at her place last night. Late. Somehow he had got to know there was trouble and went there to ask.'

'And that was when you got the wreath?'

155

Charmian looked at where Rewley had placed it on her desk. 'I suppose it had better go to HG for inspection. There might be fingerprints but I doubt if they will help. I'd say it was lifted from the crematorium or a cemetery and the funeral had been a few days ago.'

They drank some more coffee, then Rewley went off. Charmian dealt with some routine tasks, made a few telephone calls, received several, then cancelled a visit to London.

Humphrey was already in that city, he had left early with a cautionary word to her before he left. 'Keep out of the Bailey affair, leave it to Horris. I don't like the feel of it, I think you might regret getting mixed up in it.' He saw her face and gave a groan. 'You aren't going to take any notice, are you?'

'I can't, I am in it, it's the job.'

'Look at what you've got: a murder years ago in horrible circumstances of a child, unsolved, but the police think they know the killer but they can't prove it; the suspect has disappeared or at any rate they don't find her. It's a bodged up job, and there's probably a reason for that if you can find it.'

Charmian looked at him gravely. 'Precisely why I am interested.'

'Not precisely, if you are being honest, but emotionally ... Now the child's head has been discovered with a dead woman, and now the girl Emily, who was not a pupil at the school but whose sister owned it, has taken herself

156

off.'

'Or been taken.'

'As you will. It's all a bloody business and I'd like you out of it.'

'Not a hope.'

They had parted lovingly; it was amazing how domestic fondness grew on you.

At the door he had paused again; 'You had a telephone call early this morning? I heard the name Yeldon.'

'Dr Yeldon wants to talk to me.'

'Then let him. He's a good man. What he wants to say must be worth hearing.'

She had given him an extra warm kiss and told herself she might and might not. Probably she would have put Dr Yeldon off, but life and Winnie Eagle arranged that she did not.

They entered together, Miss Eagle first, the more apologetic figure of Dr Yeldon second. Charmian had advance warning of their arrival from the flustered voice of her secretary in the outer room, the words 'Miss Daniels ... Must not disturb...', followed by Winifred's commanding 'Nonsense'. No one said 'Nonsense' like Miss Eagle, she came over like one of the stronger and most articulate ladies in a Shaw play. Indeed, Charmian had wondered if she had been an actress in one of her earlier manifestations. She claimed to have had several lives, and there were times when Charmian came close to believing her. Hearing her clear tones today uttering the words

157

'Justice and Priority', she could see her as Lady Britomart, say, or even St Joan; and seeing her march through the door in her tweeds and knickerbockers, Charmian felt she might have been George Bernard Shaw himself in one of those lives. But did the time-scales match? How old was Winifred? Impossible to tell.

'Charmian!' As Winnie swept in and Dr Yeldon slid in after her, Charmian thought: No, not Bernard Shaw but Sherlock Holmes and Dr Watson. 'I need to talk to you and Billy here feels the same. We are concerned about Emily, we have both heard that she is missing.'

'Yes, I suppose you would have heard.'

'After all, you did ask us, Birdie and me, to look after the girl, I feel I can claim an interest.'

'But you haven't come just to say that.'

From where she sat, Charmian could see down the street where Dr Yeldon's car was parked with Maud Yeldon sitting in it like a sergeant-major. Poor Dr Yeldon, between Winifred and his wife, his freedom for action must be limited. From what little she had seen of Maud Yeldon, she found her alarming.

'My wife didn't want me to come, she thinks I am fussing. You won't find her, she said. They are too clever for that.'

'She said that, did she?'

'Yes, however she drove us here. I don't drive any longer ... little trouble with my eyesight.'

And Winifred uses a broomstick, of course.

'Last night we had a meeting of all those who still remember the school and the terrible events there. The Bailey family had and still has friends, even if the only ones of them left are Emily and a cousin in Scotland. She has her own importance and significance.' He was being wordy and Winifred shifted irritably in her seat. 'If it hadn't been for her, the basement room might never have been opened up. Not for many more years, I don't believe Emily would have done it alone. My belief is that a prohibition was laid upon her by her sister. I think she promised.'

'You think so?' Charmian said absently.

'She more or less said so to me when I charged her once with leaving the house to decay when so many people are homeless.'

'Wonder that place did not have squatters in it.' Winifred put in her piece.

'I believe they did for a few weeks once ... Young couple with a child ... moved out when they heard what had happened there.'

'About Emily,' said Charmian. 'I know nothing more. Superintendent Horris is the man in charge. He may tell you more.' Or he may not, Horris not being one to pass on information.

'I went round to the house last night, our little meeting had heard there was police activity ... No one was there but a very offhand young man. I came back and I told my wife that I could not leave it there.'

159

And he was not going to if he could help it, Charmian could see as much. She looked at Winifred.

'We cannot, you know,' Winifred said. 'Birdie and I are doing what we can … meditating, trying to tap into Emily's mind … Birdie was up all night, she is resting this morning, which is why she is not with us now.'

'No message came through?' said Charmian with sympathy; she had had experience of Birdie and her mind messages, they worked better with dogs than humans and she had twice got a message that Benjy was parked outside a bitch's house in Woodside. Not so good with cats, in fact no good at all, cats seemed to be what Birdie called 'naturally thick-brained', impervious, in other words.

'No message, just a sensation of discomfort, evil,' said Winnie gravely. 'Which is why I am here now. The girl is in trouble, she may be in pain.'

Charmian thought about the blood. Very likely Emily was suffering, she thought. She might be dead or dying. How long did it take you to make up a loss of blood?

Winnie looked at Dr Yeldon with meaning.

'Yes, it is why I am here too,' he said. 'At our meeting last night…' he broke off in a way which Winnie for one plainly found maddening. 'Yes, it is certainly heavy on my mind.'

Winnie said briskly: 'Come on, Billy, out
160

with it, or I will. You aren't in medical practice now, dealing with a matter of confidence.'

Billy Yeldon plunged in: 'At our meeting, Eddy Bell said that, told us...'

'Under pressure from Eleanor Fraser,' put in Winifred. 'I wouldn't call him keen to tell us.'

Charmian waited patiently.

'Eddy told us that Emily had told him that she feared for herself ... she thought someone was after her.'

Charmian absorbed the news, and looked down at the virgin blotter on her desk. She favoured a strong red blotting-paper and these days of word-processors and faxes, fewer and fewer letters arrived on it to be blotted.

Emily had probably been justified in her fears.

'So who was after her? Did Eddy say?' Or would he say, if Charmian herself questioned him? What sort of a witness was he? Better tell H. G. Horris too.

'Didn't say ... but we think, I think, that it might be Margaret Drue.'

There it was again, that name, that figure in the shadows.

'We know that she is not the dead woman ... word has got around. I take it is right, this story that it is some other person? But a woman?'

'Yes,' said Charmian.

'Not identified?' This was Winifred.

'Not yet,' said Charmian.

'Maybe never?'

'I think that is unlikely.' This was the professional police line always and, give or take a few unlucky corpses, true.

'Of course, I expect you know a lot you are not telling us.'

'Not a lot.'

Outside, she could see Maud Yeldon get out of the car to pace up and down the pavements. 'Your wife is getting impatient.'

'Born that way,' said Winifred. She stood up. 'But I suppose we should go ... Come on, Billy, we've done what we came to do ... told Charmian and stirred things up a bit.'

'Oh, is that what you came to do?'

'It is occasionally necessary,' said Winifred with dignity. 'And a citizen's right.'

And a witch's absolute necessity, Charmian thought, stirring things up.

'But there is one other thing...' Here she offered to Charmian her crocodile smile, testimony to the skill of her dentist. 'Billy, this is for you ... the tape. Hand it over.'

Dr Yeldon began to fumble in his pockets. 'Not this one, nor that ... where did I put it, Winifred? Perhaps I gave it to Maud.'

'Heaven help you, Billy,' said Winifred with detachment.

'Ah, here it is. I have it.'

'What is this?' Charmian took the tape from him. It was a home production, she could see that much.

'It's a little thing I do,' said Dr Yeldon with a seraphic smile. 'I like to have my tape-recorder for important occasions ... I picked up the habit in the surgery when it was sometimes very valuable to be able to go back and listen to the patient's voice and description of his or her symptoms ... All confidential, of course, I destroyed them at the proper time. I picked up odd noises as well that could be useful in knowing what was going on in the surgery,' he added thoughtfully. 'Amazingly sensitive some of these machines ... I suppose you could call it bugging the surgery,' he ended wistfully. 'Is that illegal?'

Charmian shook her head. 'Not as far as I know.'

'Get on with it, Billy,' said Winifred.

Thus prompted, Dr Yeldon said that what he had handed over was a tape of their meeting. He thought she might like to have it, to hear for herself what Eddy had said about Emily's fears, and judge. 'Winifred says that Eddy is a liar, I don't think he is.'

'A bit of one,' said Winifred.

Charmian looked at the tape: Street Party, it said, with yesterday's date. 'If you think it important, then Superintendent Horris should have it.'

'Not approachable,' said Billy Yeldon. 'You are. There is that man Towers, but then he is part of the scene to my mind.'

A shrewd observation, Charmian thought.

163

'And not too stable,' said the medical man, giving judgement. 'Sorry to say it but I think so.'

Shrewd again, Charmian thought, but she did not comment.

'Right, I will listen to it, and let him have it. Agreed? And I will talk to Eddy Bell myself.'

In a secret, gleeful kind of way, she knew she did not mind interfering with HG.

Maud Yeldon was still pacing up and down.

Winifred stood up. 'Let me know when you hear anything about Emily.'

'Certainly. I'm sorry I dragged you and Birdie into it.'

'Don't be silly. I knew the girl. Glad to help. Hope she turns up.' She added bluntly: 'And in one piece.'

Charmian watched them leave, and stood at the window to see all three of them drive off, Maud Yeldon driving. A memory stirred. 'Knew her once. Think I did,' she mused. 'It'll come back.' Memory worked like that, you couldn't switch it on at will but when you were least expecting it, then there the missing answer was.

She took the tape out to her secretary. 'Get this copied, then give me the copy, and send the original round to Superintendent Horris in the Incident Room. Put a note in with it to say that Dr Yeldon left it with me, because he thought I might be interested.'

'Of course, Miss Daniels, straight away.' She

164

had a pleasant voice this new girl, Charmian thought, and nice smile.

'And the wreath . . . have you sent it round to the Superintendent for inspection?'

'I rang him up and he said to send it straight round to the Forensic Laboratory . . . he was going to there himself, but he doesn't expect anything from it. Thinks it just a silly joke by someone.'

'Right, I'll have the copy of the tape when it's ready.'

She went back into her own room to deal with the routine stuff already piling up. Two anxious and not totally normal men on my hands, she thought as she signed letters. Jim Towers, and George Rewley, both for different reasons not quite themselves.

It was late afternoon when HG telephoned. 'Didn't get much from that florist wreath . . . don't suppose you expected it, but the lab boys have found nothing except traces of other flowers. Nicked from a grave somewhere, they think, and so do I.'

'I agree.'

'I'd say some bugger's silly joke, but it has to be someone who knew Emily Bailey was missing, so the jury is still out on that one. If I have any great thoughts I will let you know. Do the same for me, will you?'

'Unless she sent it herself.'

He was silent for a moment. 'A weird scenario if so, but the whole thing is weird. Are

165

you serious?'

'Not sure.'

She heard him draw in a breath, and there were noises off: men talking, telephones ringing. He was back in the Incident Room.

'I can tell you something: the child's head . . .' Yes, that had been worrying her . . . 'It had been kept under refrigeration. Frozen, in short.'

'Boiled first, then refrigerated?'

'The other way round, he thinks. Probably done in the stove in the Bailey basement. Yes, not nice, is it, but the heads that the old public hangmen boiled in the Morbid Kitchen and then put on display were cooked with various salts in the water. Our Joey, whoever, hadn't got such. Or didn't know how. But did have a freezer. That's modern times for you.'

'I wonder why it had to be kept?'

'Who knows? Just for company, maybe. That's what they say, isn't it?'

'And where?'

'That's the question. Find that out and we will be on the way to a lot of answers, but the forensics are going to try for traces of where it might have been. So let's keep hoping. By the way, thanks for the tape, I haven't played it yet.'

'I don't know what use it will be.'

'Worth a try.' HG was being very jovial for him. 'One other thing: it seemed that the body of the woman had been in situ maybe in the

166

cupboard, probably elsewhere, somewhere she got wood dust on her, for years. She was dried, a mummy, because of the conditions there.'

'Do you mean she was there when the Baileys boarded up the room?'

'No, probably not. Because I had the boarding checked and although Eddy Bell had made a fair hash of it with his chisel, it looks as though it had been taken down and put up again more than once.' He added by way of explanation, 'Marks on the wood, holes, scrapes, that sort of thing.'

'That is interesting. Good work, HG.'

'It's not exactly a big step forward, but it sort of fills in the picture. Oh, one other thing: I have sent Jim Towers on leave. He came in today looking a total wreck and I sent him off.'

Charmian absorbed this news. 'You probably did the right thing.'

'I know I did.' HG did not mention Dolly Barstow, but he certainly knew of the relationship. 'You will get all the reports and all in the regular way of business.'

'I have been pondering on the identity of the woman whose body was found,' she began.

'Nothing on her body of much help,' said the Superintendent cautiously, 'except the newspaper cutting with a picture of you and the message. It suggests certain things.'

It does indeed, thought Charmian, apart from the fact she knew my name. If the message was a message and was meant for me.

167

'Can I come round and talk to you?'

'Certainly, ma'am.' HG was suddenly more formal. 'Delighted to have you. Or I could come to you?'

'I'll walk over to the Incident Room.'

It was a warm afternoon and she wanted some air. The path of the Incident Room (now transferred from the van outside the old Bailey house in Flanders Street where it had started out) lay across one quiet back road and into a paved yard. The yard was full of parked cars through which she threaded her way.

Once you have seen one incident room, you have seen them all, she reflected as she pushed open the door, yet each does have its own peculiar flavour.

Smell, really.

Since H. G. Horris was a committed non-smoker, urging the same in all who worked for him and with him, this room was not so heavily laden with cigarette smoke as some she had known. But it didn't smell of flowers either. Instead, it smelt of men sweating slightly, with a tinge of aftershave.

Someone had been brewing coffee, she could smell that, and there was a mug of it on HG's desk, although it looked cold and had a skin on it. He was standing by it, talking to a shirt-sleeved detective whose face she knew. Farmelow, she thought, was his name, and his rank that of sergeant. He knew her too, and straightened himself and put on an alert, friendly look which might be assumed. She was not always welcome.

HG swung round and smiled. It was one of his smiles into which you need not read too much of friendliness, more a desire to get on with the job by settling for easy relations. He could be aggressive and quarrelsome, as she very well knew, but he was not about to show that side to her at this moment. Possibly never, but equally possibly he could do so if he felt she was in his way: he knew how to fight for his territory. But so did she, she reflected; she had struggled her way up the career ladder, receiving bruises as well as handing some back.

You never warmed to HG, but you did trust him. Now he came forward, not introducing Farmelow, who knew his place and melted away into it: he was a background figure at the moment although what he had been saying to the Superintendent might have been important, and she thought it had been.

'Let's talk,' and HG drew her into a corner where two chairs had been strategically placed. 'I expect you are thinking what I am thinking: why was the woman planted there, in that cupboard in that basement in that house?'

'Not to mention why was the child's head there too.'

'Exactly. When it looked as though the dead woman was Margaret Drue, then the answer looked easy. Well, easier: it was a revenge killing.'

169

'Yes,' Charmian nodded. 'And either the dead woman had the head of the child and it went in with her as the child's killer or her killer' ... she paused ... 'her killer somehow had or discovered the head independently and put it there.' Another pause. 'But if the dead woman is not Drue, as now appears, why was she killed, and why put there with the head? It complicates things, doesn't it?'

'She may have been the child's killer with Drue innocent. No trace of Drue yet,' he added gloomily. 'Nor, for that matter, of the girl Emily, but I am more hopeful there. She hasn't been gone long, somehow I think she will be back. It was human blood in the room, by the way, that was what Farmelow had for me there. And her blood group, but the blood group of a lot of other people too.'

HG did lumber up to a point, Charmian thought, so she put it to him first. 'But this must be what we are all thinking: the woman in the cupboard has to have had some connection with the child Alana and the school.'

HG nodded. 'Sure.'

'And there are several women connected with the school, who worked there or were married to those who did. But only one of them is not around now.'

HG nodded. 'Madelaine Mason.'

Madelaine Mason, who had been the matron and taught at the school.

'I thought of her too,' said Charmian. 'What
170

happened to her after the murder? The school closed, she no longer had a job.'

'We are working on it. Her address was on the files, 3 Waverly Street, Merrywick, but she has not been there since two weeks after the school closed. There was a note in the file that she was doing teaching for the local council schools.'

'Who must know her movements.'

'She last worked for them over nine years ago,' said Horris tersely. 'In fact, just about the time she left her rented flat in Merrywick and left no address.'

They looked at each other.

'And so far,' said Horris, 'we have no further tracing of her.'

'So it could be her in the cupboard?'

HG nodded. 'My guess too. We are working on it. But I have got a photograph of her. In colour, too.' He leaned across the table and extracted a photograph from a manila folder.

'Where did you get it?'

'She left it behind, unpaid for, at a local photographer's.'

He had been hard at work, Charmian thought, and deserved a slight play of smugness around his eyes.

It was the photograph of a tall, well-built woman in early middle age, with well-cut hair; she was wearing a pleated, striped skirt in light apricot with a white shirt. The hair, Charmian remembered, had been cut by her own friend and hairdresser, Baby: Beryl Andrea Barker.

'We think that the face and body shown here match with what we have. We think we have a match.'

Charmian nodded slowly, still studying the photograph. 'I remember skirts like that, we were all wearing them that year, stripes in different colours. I had one myself, in dark blue.'

She stood there while she looked at the picture and assembled her thoughts. The dead woman had held a piece of newspaper secretly about her person, she had written on it what sounded like a plea for help. The newspaper was not absolutely fresh from the press in all probability when she wrote on it with a pencil; it had been folded and refolded more than once. An old scrap, possibly in any handbag or briefcase she might have carried. None had been found, though. So a newspaper where she was at the time?

That was the point, wasn't it? Where she was. You do not use an oldish scrap of newsprint when you have free access to any better. Charmian followed the thought through: she did not have free access, she was not free. She was imprisoned. Madelaine Mason had been imprisoned before being killed.

Charmian looked down and seemed to see that prison: small, cold and dark. Yes, it must have been dark, but not totally without light because the dead woman, Madelaine Mason, if it was truly she, had been able to scrawl a message on a piece of paper. My message, to me, Charmian thought. So either the imprisoned woman had had the paper on her, or she had found it where she was shut up; in the same way, either she had the pencil about her person or there had been one where she could use it.

Two things followed logically from that: she had not been tied up, and she had not been watched. Or not all the time. That meant, then, that the prison was very safe. It must have been terrifying, and she knew that the woman had been terrified.

She raised her eyes to H. G. Horris. 'She was a prisoner, and I think she knew she was going to be killed.'

'I'd have to be convinced about that,' he said sceptically. 'It's guessing, questions to be answered there.'

'Then ask the questions and try to get answers. Where was she imprisoned? Where was she killed? Was it where she was imprisoned? And was it where her body was found?'

A lot of questions inside questions there, she thought, and still left was the biggest of all. Why was she killed?

'For sure she isn't going to sit up and tell us,' said HG somewhat sourly.

'No, but her body might.' Charmian

173

couldn't keep out the crack of the whip in her voice. Let him be obstructive and dour, but let him get on with it. 'Get all forensic traces— shreds, fibres, hairs, bits of skin, traces of colour off her clothes, hair, hands.'

HG admitted she was right: 'Yes, I'll consult the miracle workers.'

'One more thing...' she paused, but better get on with it. She wished she could have introduced it easily, that it had sprung naturally out of the conversation, because she knew that he did not like Rewley. Rewley was neither liked nor trusted in that group, as being too clever by half, and able to lip-read, which naturally made him suspect in that secretive society. She took the plunge. 'George Rewley...' and at once she saw HG's face change... What's coming now, she could read, so let him have it. 'He has information about more human remains...'

'Where?'

This was the weak part. 'Not known yet, but he expects to find out... he believes, we believe, it is connected with this case.'

HG let out a long melodious whistle, he was a musical man, which he then turned into a low groan. 'Isn't it marvellous? Get one corpse and they start coming out of the woodwork. Who is it this time, not the girl Emily?'

'Well, we hope not, don't we?' said Charmian in a level voice.

'I'm counting on her being alive.'

174

'I hope she is, but she has to be found.'

'Sometimes girls like that just reappear,' said HG cynically.

'So they do, but not always ... Let me say something. I think that the dead woman was kept imprisoned somewhere. Look for somewhere small, with not much light, but enough to read and write by, a room tucked away where no one could hear a voice calling for help. Possibly a shed or a garage, but not too near people. Yet near enough to Flanders Street so that the woman and the head, don't forget the head, could be put there. She might not have been dead ... As the head had been kept under refrigeration, the place I am imagining can't be out in the wilds ... It will be in Windsor, possibly somewhere in the centre of the town ... that's what I think. Look for that place.'

Horris thought without pleasure of the resources he had at his command, not too many men when all was said, and he thought too of the operations already on hand: a robbery in the Castle (where no robbery ever should happen), an attempted rape in the Great Park, a mugging on the down platform at the railway station, and sighed. 'We can try.'

'And when you find it,' she said crisply, 'that will be the prison where Madelaine Mason was held.'

'Have a go,' conceded Horris.

'And it will probably be where Emily is now.'

175

CHAPTER EIGHT

So that was how it was going to be, thought Charmian. HG was doing his best, but didn't want her interfering; nor did he think she was being helpful. She walked back into her office in a thoughtful mood, hoping that the short walk back would clear her mind and lead to fruitful thought. But it did not.

When she considered the town of Windsor with its many old mansions and houses, all with outbuildings of differing sorts, the many coach-houses and stables, not to mention garages and sheds, she could understand his gloom at her request for a search. As well as Windsor itself, there was the outer suburb of Merrywick and going towards London that part of the conurbation nearest Windsor which was Cheasey. In Cheasey anything could happen and anything be hidden. One just had to hope the killer of Madelaine Mason was not an inhabitant of Cheasey.

No, she thought, it was not the style of a true Cheasey man to dispose of his bodies in Windsor; if he had one it would be safer in Cheasey. Indeed, there were probably any number of bodies laid about in Cheasey that she knew nothing about. Never would know anything with any luck.

All the same, this was not a Cheasey murder.

They were a rough but straightforward lot there, their murders had no subtlety and were easily traced home. In fact, since the criminal circles of Cheasey (and there were precious few others) were made up of clan groups, the murders usually were what you could call home or domestic murders: they killed each other. Brother, cousin, spouse, it made no odds, Clytemnestra would have felt quite comfortable in Cheasey and, indeed, found strong competition.

No, this was not a Cheasey murder. It was complicated and terrible and dark. A Windsor murder, in short. Windsor was a town with a history into which this crime could be fitted.

She stood up and walked around the room, touching her books, looking out of the window.

Place was important, she was sure of that, the place where Madelaine had been imprisoned and where she had been killed, where the head had been kept, this place was important. Hard to locate though; certainly she had blithely presented H. G. Horris and his team with a difficult problem. She wasn't sure if he was really going to look, or not hard, nor could she blame him. She could pull rank and force to be very active, but in her time she herself had had insuperable problems thrust at her on a plate. As a consequence, she knew she was not going to push HG.

Think about it yourself, dear, she said.

Think of it as a historical or an archaeological problem ... You are Schliemann looking for a site of Mycenae and the grave of Agamemnon; you are Arthur Evans searching for the Minoan shrines of Crete. You are that young man you met at a party in London who is trying to find out if and where the Romans bridged the Thames. You are a group of early medievalists trying to prove that the Vikings landed in North America. Eric the Red, step forward.

No, it was no good, her mind was not working that way today; worse, she had the uneasy impression that it never would on this particular problem. Or perhaps it was true what people said: that happy married life, or even worse, motherhood, addled the brain.

She turned back to work, she would not be brain-damaged. In such a mood it was best to stick to routine. And after all, she need not be involved in the case.

Later, she put down what she was reading, she was making nonsense of it anyway, a report of London's traffic as a security problem. Damn it all, she was involved. The woman who died had called on her for help. Ten years too late, it was up to her to deliver it.

She went to her window to look out. She couldn't see much of the town, but there was the top of the Castle with the Royal Standard visible to those with long sight, which meant that the Queen herself was in residence. A

178

helicopter would be the thing, she thought, sailing over the town, observing all likely buildings, then photographing them. The force had a helicopter but it was usually in use checking either traffic or royal security. The Queen had her own fleet, of course, perhaps she would lend one.

The idea diverted Charmian for a moment, and she considered it with amusement. There it would go, the royal helicopter, imperially furnished, possibly emblazoned with the royal arms, seeking out a murderer. The headlines in the newspapers would be a delight. She had no doubt that Her Majesty would agree if the request ever reached her, but of course it would not. Charmian knew only too well the many layers of authority that would step in to bar such a request. In a matter of life and death, the answer would certainly be yes; to hunt down a killer's prison, probably no.

One could not be quite sure, nothing about the Court could ever be taken for granted, but Charmian thought she had the psychology right.

She went back to her desk. If misery sharpened the wits, then her best bet at the moment was Rewley, with Dolly Barstow and Jim Towers as runners-up. Towers, of course, was off the case, and Dolly was only on it if she asked to be, and Charmian agreed.

With a special request of H. G. Horris for co-operation? This he would be obliged to give

179

but might do so slowly and grudgingly. She knew the man and knew him to be honest, not very open-minded (although sharp-eyed and observant when it so suited him) and not in favour of women operating on his patch.

She had heard, though, that he liked Dolly Barstow, and that Dolly had been known to say kind words about him.

Perhaps it would be quicker and easier to ask Winifred and Birdie for a bit of co-operative witchcraft: crystal-gazing or a reading from the tea-leaves. And didn't Winifred go in for a bit of hypnotherapy? No laughter, please. It was never a game to them, they were too serious and high-minded for that. Birdie might consent to do a reading when holding a scrap of material from the victim or to join hands with Winifred and try some telepathic communication. But no, she could send her thought-waves out into the blue and Charmian had no idea where to direct her.

She might try looking for Emily that way. Either it would work or it wouldn't. Charmian was a natural sceptic, but she had to admit when Muff the cat had been lost once, she had been sufficiently worried to hold hands with Birdie and Winifred while concentrating on Muff. She herself had seen nothing, but Birdie had seen a deep hole with wood on the top, which had turned out to be a neighbour's coal-hole (the Maid of Honour Row houses were so old-fashioned that they still had coal-holes, even though life elsewhere had long since moved on to bunkers and even oil central heating), and Muff had indeed been in the coal-hole, cross, hungry and all her own fault for mouse hunting without due care. The dead mouse, partly eaten, was in there with her.

True it was, that Charmian might have found the cat in the coal-hole anyway since Muff was letting out shrill cries at intervals, but she had given Birdie thanks for setting her on the way. Birdie had received the thanks most regally, too. Now she thought about it, had not Birdie insisted she hold a few of Muff's hairs (Muff left them all over the place, so there was no problem there) in her hand?

Charmian pushed the idea aside. This was not how the well-trained police mind thought. She could imagine HG's face if she said: well, my private witchcraft source tells me that ...

She never finished the sentence, because there was a knock on the door, which opened at once before Dolly Barstow. Dolly did, it is true, hover on the threshold for a second as if she knew that was not how you burst in on ma'am even if she was your friend, but she was in a hurry and did not mind showing it.

'I was thinking about you,' said Charmian, swinging round in her chair in welcome. 'Perhaps there is something in telepathy ... I was thinking of sending you over Windsor in a helicopter.'

Dolly ignored this, taking it as a flight of

181

fancy. 'Jim's been given leave, forcible leave . . . with a suggestion he see his doctor and claim a rest on medical grounds. I'm furious.'

'I can see you are.' Charmian swung her chair back, no longer feeling so welcoming. 'Did you have anything to do with it?'

'Certainly not.' Not quite true; she had not made the suggestion, but she had certainly concurred in the idea that it was a good thing to keep Jim Towers away from too close a connection with Alana's head, just as you would keep an adolescent schoolboy, not quite settled in his sexuality, away from the part of Juliet in a school production of Shakespeare's tragedy of young love if Romeo was too taking a young lad. Some separations are made for the good of everyone.

'He's very upset . . . it won't do his career any good.'

Charmian took a deep breath. 'Are you in love with him, Dolly? Or perhaps I should say: how much?'

'I knew you'd ask that . . . or something like it. You've been working up to it for weeks.'

'Have I?' Charmian was surprised. 'I'm not sure if I think about you as much as all that, Dolly. Perhaps less than you imagine. I have had other problems on my mind.'

Dolly flushed. 'Yes, sorry. There are certain states that make you paranoid, and I'm a bad case at the moment.'

'But when I do think of you, I am fond of

182

you.' Although that might not continue if you go on being aggressive to me.

'And as to being in love, I don't know. I'm not sure what I feel about him. And I'm pretty sure he's in the same state. State of flux,' she said unhappily.

'I think he is better off the case, and you may not be right about his career ... might not do him harm. HG is a decent sort, he won't put in a bad report.'

'I know, and he's made it sound good, suggested that Jim get on with the book he is writing ... or thinking of writing ... I don't know if he has actually written a word.' Her voice trailed away. 'The Head and the Killer.' Was that really a book she wanted the man to write? 'Yes, he has been decent.'

Charmian looked at her with sympathy; although they were friends they did not usually exchange emotional confidences, and perhaps they had already gone as far down that path as they should.

'I don't think I have quite got over Kate's death,' went on Dolly. 'I miss her. That's why I moved into where I am now ... no memories there.'

'I understand. I miss her too.'

'It's worse for you, I only got to know her when she settled down a bit and came back here to live. But we sort of bonded. Did you know she left me a bit of her jewellery ... a necklace I always admired. I don't know if I

183

can ever bear to wear it, as it is, I can hardly look at it.'

'How's Rewley? He doesn't open up to me.'

'Not to anyone.' A pause. 'He's not happy.'

'No,' said Charmian. 'Of course not. You aren't, nor am I. It's not to be expected.'

'But he would be a lot happier if he had more contact with his child. Or if the child was not so much richer than he was. It gives Anny control. Money is a bloody nuisance.'

'Not to have any might be worse; he took on that problem when he married Kate. And don't be too hasty about Anny. I think when he is in more control of himself, you will find Anny reasonable. She'll hand that child over.'

'Do you think so?'

'I do,' said Charmian, hoping she was right. 'Have you seen him today?'

'In passing; he looked as if he had his mind elsewhere. But he said he was working on something. Or did he say someone?'

'Both, I expect. Where is Jim Towers now?'

'Packing his things, to move out of that grotty flat he lives in to move in with me.' There was a defiant sound in Dolly's voice.

'He's moving in with you?'

'Into my equally grotty place.' No doubt about the defiance. 'He needs a protector.'

'And that is you?'

'For the time being. Not for ever. Probably not for long.'

'What's he going to do, after he's moved his

bags?'

'He's going up to Harrogate to consult a friend who's great in forensics. I suppose they will talk heads.'

Charmian was thoughtful. 'He has a genuine subject there, you know, if he can keep it on the rails.'

'I know that. Which is why I am helping.'

'No promises, but there might be a place for him in the team. When he's got himself together.'

It was not a suggestion made without forethought, nor entirely disinterested: working together might force them apart rather than draw them together, and she thought she wanted to do this. So it was painful to see Dolly's flush of pleasure. Traitor you, she thought. 'What brings you here now?'

Dolly was glad to change the subject, especially as she intended to turn the spotlight on to Charmian. 'Apart from the fact, which you may not have noticed, that it is now early evening, and the end of my working day, I wonder if you have noticed that there is a police helicopter flying over the town? In fact, you can hear it now.' She held up her hand. 'Listen.'

Charmian went to the window, from which she could see an expanse of sky, and yes, there was the helicopter. Good for HG, he had thought of it for himself.

'I suppose it's looking for Emily?'

185

Charmian stood surveying the sky, overhung and misty. 'Yes, or somewhere she might be hidden. Imprisoned.'

Dolly raised an eyebrow. 'Will it do much good?'

'Possibly not, or not today. There's one of those river mists coming down, but there will be photographs, I hope, which can be studied later.'

'What about Margaret Drue? Is she being sought for murder, and now possibly for abducting Emily?'

'She's in the frame,' said Charmian, going back to her desk, as the helicopter hovered westward over the city towards Slough. 'But it won't be easy. Good to get track of her, though.'

'It won't be easy. She must have changed her appearance, don't you think?'

Charmian looked into the distance as if she could see Margaret Drue there, staring back. Then she said: 'Oh yes, she will have changed ... perhaps we will hardly know her.'

Dolly had her own strong reactions to the thought; there was this woman, whom they might not recognize, probably would not, and yet she was a killer, who might be still willing, and wanting, to kill. 'Nasty feeling that she's on the prowl wreaking havoc.'

Charmian stood up and reached for her briefcase and handbag.

This looked decisive, Dolly thought. 'What

186

are you going to do now?'

To her surprise, Charmian looked amused. 'Something wicked...'

'I can't believe that.'

'It depends where you are standing.' Charmian sounded amused.

'Can I come with you?'

Charmian considered. 'Yes, why not?'

*　　*　　*

The house where Emily had lived now had a police presence. Two police cars stood outside the door, parked by the kerb, preventing, to their fury, the parking of the cars of several local householders. An unmarked police car, but clearly identifiable to those in the know, stood further up the road, thus impeding at least one other owner of a Residents' Only parking permit. Charmian, seeing all this, was careful to put her car round the corner.

The door was locked, but was opened by a uniformed WPC before she could ring the bell.

'No press,' said the girl.

Charmian was getting out her identification without a word when a detective whom she knew appeared. 'Hello, ma'am, you coming in?'

'If I may. Bender, isn't it?' This was a question to which the answer had to be yes, as she had every intention of entering. Accordingly, the detective made none, but stood aside politely.

'Yes, ma'am, we met over the Merrywick murder, if you remember...'

'No news about the girl?'

'Nothing fresh, not that I know of. We've just been going over everything in the room, searching for some clue where she might be.'

Dolly Barstow inserted herself into the house, which seemed stuffier and colder than last night; she moved behind Charmian as unobtrusively as she could, hoping to avoid all comment. She too knew Detective-Sergeant Bender with whom she had once been on exceedingly friendly terms. Their eyes met, but he said nothing, although as he put it later: I passed a message across that she could read if she wanted. The message said I have happy memories and am still around. But he had heard she had other business on now. Too bad.

Dolly had kept quiet on the journey round, asking no questions, but watching Charmian's face. If this was wicked business, then she would learn more by observation than speech. She had not been surprised as they drew up close to where Emily had lodged, but she could not see what was wicked about it. True, H. G. Horris would probably not be best pleased if Charmian was still on what he probably called 'the interference racket' but he would hold his tongue and any sniping comments would be passed later to his pals. If he had any. Rumour had it that he was not a popular man.

Charmian walked into Emily's bedsitting room which now looked even worse than last night. True, the blood had been cleared away from the basin, but the dustiness and smears left on wood and china and on glass in the fingerprinting exercise, which appeared to have gone on with great thoroughness, made their own contribution to the mess.

Charmian stood for a moment on the threshold. The room was empty, except for the WPC who stood by the basin as if she was keeping guard. The sergeant had not followed them in, but gone out of the house towards his car, where he planned to have a quiet smoke. Around Charmian, as he knew, there was a permanent no-smoking zone.

Charmian gave Dolly an oblique look and nodded towards the girl. Your job, the look said, is to keep her occupied. Dolly got the message, she had worked with Charmian before; fortunately she knew what to do.

'Any chance of a cuppa,' she murmured to the girl. 'I'm parched.'

The WPC flushed with pleasure. 'Sure. I know where to make it. The landlord here is a decent chap and showed me the kettle. I've been here all day and needed something myself. Help yourself, he said, but I didn't take him up on that. It's my tea and milk, of course, I wouldn't poach,' she added virtuously.

Dolly followed the WPC into the kitchen on the ground floor. 'I don't think you'll go far in

189

the force, dear,' she murmured under her breath, 'you're too trusting, but you have a lovely nature.'

Left alone, Charmian kept an eye on the sergeant outside in his car, while she moved round the room. You could tell a lot about a person from their room, and this room told her that Emily took her studies seriously, had a few good clothes but not many, did not smoke, drank a little wine, but probably did not take any drugs. The room didn't smell druggy. And now the blood had gone, all it smelt of was police bodies, and even that smell was fading.

Here were her pile of books. Charmian flipped them over: Pollock and Maitland, Plucknett's *Concise History of English Law*, Faversham on the British Constitution, and several political biographies in paperback. Yes, she took her work seriously.

No sign of a boyfriend, no letters and no photographs. Well, that didn't mean anything, she may not have been a girl for mementos. Charmian went quickly through the drawers in the desk, which revealed just writing-paper in neat piles, some written essays in one, but no letters, and no diary. She must have had a diary, unless she had nothing to record or carried all engagements in her head.

Nothing in the dressing-table drawers but clean underclothes and tights. No condoms, no birth control pills. So she was either celibate or chancing it. A sparse life.

190

Charmian picked up the picture of the school group once again; she was surprised to see it still here, but presumably it had been fingerprinted. Her own thoughts were on the bleak side, she could blame herself: I ought to have observed you more closely when we were together. But you were just a girl I met and who asked me to help.

One last quick look around, because the sergeant had finished his smoke and was on the way. Hanging up on the door was an old blue dressing-gown, and the waste-paper basket had not been emptied.

Dolly came back in with a mug; she held it to Charmian with an expressionless face. 'Have a cup of tea.'

'That wasn't so wicked,' said Dolly.

'No, not wicked at all, just a joke.'

No, that wasn't so wicked, Charmian said to herself as she dropped Dolly back by her own car and drove off. This was wicked: she patted her pocket in which a slip of paper with Emily's handwriting was tucked away. Only a slip, unimportant, it had been in the waste-paper basket, but she had a use for it. Also in her pocket was a handkerchief from Emily's dressing-gown pocket. Not clean, in fact distinctly grubby. Well used. But that suited her purpose.

And even this is not so very wicked, Charmian told herself. Now comes the wicked bit, which I will never confess to. Ever. If

191

anything comes of it, in the way of consummate detective work, I will never ever admit to it. She was half amused at herself, and a little surprised, and underneath uneasy. Or was it queasy? Something of that too.

*   *   *

She parked her car outside her own house, checked inside to see if her husband was home (he was not), then walked round to where the witches lived. Muff watched her go from a tree in the garden.

Birdie opened the door to her, her hair hanging loose on her shoulders. It was also dripping wet.

'Oh sorry, you've just washed your hair.'

Birdie, always dignified, held the door open. 'No matter, come in. Winifred will be pleased to see you. I think she was hoping you would call. As I was myself.'

'Hoping', in witch speak, often meant that they had been quietly musing upon Charmian and willing her to do what was desired. With a pang, she thought that after all it had not been free will, or wickedness, that had brought her here, but a strong push of hoping.

Even as the thought came, Winifred appeared wrapped in a towelling robe; her hair also was wet. Perhaps you had to be wet to achieve a good impetus to your hoping. Winifred held a curly red wig in her hand, also wet. 'Here's your wig, Birdie. Take it from me, will you? Ah, thanks ... Good to see you, Charmian dear, I was hoping you'd come.'

'So I understand.'

'Now, no cynicism dear, it doesn't become you, as my dear mother used to say.' She smiled, her teeth yellow and strong and very even. Were they her own teeth, Charmian wondered, or a spare set, perhaps inserted for the occasion; she had never noticed them before. What occasion then? 'Don't think I can't read your thoughts, because I can. Not always, I concede that, you are a skilful masker, as you have to be, and my skills come and go, it is their nature.' She smiled again. 'Strong today.'

'You are at a peak, dear,' said Birdie with admiration. 'Your forces are running mighty strong.' She seemed sometimes to talk of Winifred as if she was a prize animal, say a horse, that Birdie was specially interested in. 'Very powerful,' she repeated.

I suppose I ought be glad of that, considering what I want of them, thought Charmian. Then she tried to repress the thought, in case Winifred read it and delivered that awful smirk.

'We are going to a Laundering,' offered Winifred. 'That is where we are bound.' She put on this somewhat archaic form of speech when it suited her. Just as she had a good variety of stable language too when needed.

193

'Oh.' Charmian had a sudden picture of rows of washing machines chugging away merrily. 'Is that why you are bathing?'

'No, the Laundering, which is the ritual cleansing before a new witch or warlock is admitted to our order, comes later, this is a Pre-wash.'

It was amazing, Charmian thought, how even the religious rituals could pick up and use commercial jargons. She looked upon the pre-washers with affection. 'Where is the Laundering then? In Windsor?' There was the river, after all, although one could never be sure how clean it was. Still, it was the idea of purification that counted not the actual dirt content of the water.

'No, near Banbury.'

That was a surprise, not what she had expected somehow. 'That's nice,' she said weakly. 'Why Banbury?'

'Not strictly Banbury, dear, but at one of the Tews not far away there is a henge, quite a small one, really hardly damaged by time at all, and very holy. I think I can say it has a great sense of sanctity. It's in a private garden, all safe. A very nice small pond close to hand for the immersion. All private, we prefer total privacy for immersions at Launderings since the body must be totally naked.'

Charmian could see the picture, and agreed with Winifred that as newly made witches and warlocks dipped in the water, it would be better to have no outsiders. 'How do you get there?' Broomsticks seemed out.

'We take the train to Oxford and then get on a bus,' said Winifred, suddenly practical.

Birdie put down the wig, which Charmian now realized she had often seen her wear without recognizing what it was. 'So what is it you want, dear? I can see you want something.'

Transparent to them today I am, decided Charmian. 'I want you to help me locate Emily.' She found herself using the word locate rather than find because somehow it seemed appropriate to the process she wanted them to use. Telepathy, could you call it? Reading the runes?

She produced from her pocket the scrap of paper with Emily's handwriting on it, and the dirty handkerchief. Thank goodness for a dirty girl, she thought. Surely it would be easier to pick up waves, emanations, call them what you will, which would summon up a picture of Emily and where she was, from possessions loaded with debris?

'I thought if I gave you these to see, or touch, or hold, you might be able to tell me where Emily is now?'

Birdie was still for a moment, then she held out her hand. It was Birdie who had this gift, if gift it was, and who would do this thing, not Winifred who provided back-up but no illumination; Winifred had other gifts, not all of them of an easy kind.

195

'Give them to me. I might be able to help,' Birdie said gravely. 'No promises. Sometimes the mind can do it and sometimes not. Sometimes it tells the truth and other times it lies. Like all human activities, it is fallible.'

'I understand that.'

'And you do not even believe in it.'

It was a time for honesty. 'Not altogether.'

'But it is worth a try ... that is what you are thinking, isn't it?'

Birdie was very serious. Charmian noticed the difference between the sometimes ironic tone in which she spoke of her witching powers, and her present manner, which confirmed what she had always thought, that although Birdie enjoyed being a witch it was more of a game or hobby to her. But with this other business she was in earnest.

'Yes.' In spite of herself, Charmian was impressed. Do I take this seriously? Perhaps I had better.

'I knew she'd come, Birdie.' Winifred was triumphant, hair still dripping, but pleased with herself. 'Told you she would. Leave it to me, I said. I'll get her.'

'Thanks, Winifred,' said Charmian, without turning her head towards Winifred. After a short session with Winifred in this mood, she felt the absence of free will. Damn you, Winnie. 'And you did. Having got me here, let's see what you two can do.'

Birdie motioned the two of them to follow

196

her into the sitting room where she took a seat at the table. She held the handkerchief and the letter in her hand, but she made no other preparations, the curtains were not drawn, nor did she shut her eyes. But she continued to look grave.

'Take my other hand, Winifred, you have power and may give me some.'

Winifred was inclined to fuss: 'What about your hair? It's all wet. Let me dry it.'

Birdie ignored her.

Charmian moved forward. 'Do you want me? Can I help?'

'No.' Birdie was still very serious. 'You are too negative.'

Winifred sat down at the table, taking Birdie's hand. Charmian took a seat facing them. For a moment she had a swift vision of H. G. Horris's face, full of horror. Then it faded, to be replaced with one of her husband's more sceptical smiles. 'Oh come,' he seemed to be saying. 'This isn't like you, you're the sceptical one.'

Would the room grow cold as Birdie concentrated? Would Birdie drift away into a trance? Charmian had not been present when Birdie had been seeking Benjy. Winifred was looking troubled, but Birdie's face was very very grave.

Silence.

Charmian moved in her chair, then stopped herself, holding her hands; she drew her feet

197

firmly together, anchoring to one spot. She wanted to cough but bit it back. She could see a drop of water slowly fall off Birdie's hair and drip down her neck. Not that anything disturbed Birdie.

Charmian had wondered if Birdie would start to moan or groan or call out as a vision came to her, but nothing happened. Five minutes, ten minutes. She could hear the clock on the wall ticking.

Then, still quietly, still seriously, Birdie began to speak. 'This place is dark. I suppose it is a room but there is little light. I smell wood, but it is not a pleasant smell, the wood is old and damp. A great dustiness in the air ... It is not far away ... Not a house, but I cannot make out what it is. But I know there is wood and oil. Yes, and stone. Certainly stone beneath her feet. Or is it brick? Perhaps both ... Dark, closed in, cold ... Emily is there. She is certainly there.'

'Is she dead?'

Birdie did not answer for a moment. 'I think not. No, I can't tell you that. These are ideas, sensations, I am dealing in, not certainties. But her presence is there.'

'And it is not far away?'

Birdie looked troubled. 'I think it must be close. It feels close ...'

All this time, she had not been looking at Charmian; now she turned to her. 'That's it, I'm afraid. Not much. But you didn't expect an address and telephone number.'

'Did it feel like a prison? As if the girl was imprisoned there?'

Birdie seemed to look inside herself, to see if she could draw out an answer. Charmian waited. But then Birdie shook her head. 'Can't say. Beyond me, that one. But I will say it feels like a bloody unpleasant place.' She drew in a sharp breath. 'Yes, it has known violence ... I can smell it.'

She began to be much less calm. 'It's a bad place, I can tell you that, Charmian.' Her hands, so steady and calm, began to shake.

'Now Birdie,' said Winifred in alarm. 'I'll get you a drink of water.'

Birdie let her go, then sipped the water. 'Sorry about this, not my style at all, and it may all be nothing but my imagination. You can't be sure.' She took another, longer drink. 'And anyway, not much help.'

'I wouldn't say that.' Charmian picked up her case and bag, ready to go. 'I'm thinking it over, Birdie, things have a way of clicking together. You know that, it's the way you move forward sometimes.' It was true, somewhere, embedded in what Birdie had come out with, was the chance of something useful.

Winnie put up her hand. 'Sit down, and I'll make us all a nice cup of tea.' She was looking anxiously at Birdie.

'No, I must go, and you've got your
199

Laundering.' Strong whisky was more Winifred's style than tea, something must have thrown her off her balance.

'No hurry about that, we have tomorrow.'

Doing what she was told, Charmian sat down while Birdie took several deep breaths. There was a bunch of roses and pinks in the room which she went over to smell as if she needed to get something, some stink, out of her nostrils.

'Sorry, Birdie.'

'Don't be. Only too glad to help. I'd like to help find the girl. Clear things up.'

Winifred returned with the tea-tray on which was also a bottle of whisky. 'That's a bad business, you're into,' she said, pouring out tea and adding generous tots of whisky too.

'That's what I think.' Charmian accepted her cup of tea, after all, the whisky was welcome and home was just around the corner; she would be walking. 'It's hard to imagine how a woman like Margaret Drue ever got a job there.'

'She had good references, I imagine,' said Winifred. 'Possibly forged, but I don't suppose it was her reference that got her the job.'

'What do you mean?'

'Oh come on.'

'No, explain.'

'She was quite a taking woman if you had the taste for that sort of thing, and Nancy did have.'

200

'I see.' Charmian put her cup on the table and sat back. 'They were lovers?'

'I don't know if it went that far.'

'I am surprised.' She was thinking. 'No hint of it got into the police files.'

'No? Oh well...'

'Who told you?'

'No one told me,' said Winifred drily. 'I didn't have to be told. I saw for myself. But they were very discreet ... I always felt there was someone else in the frame egging them on.'

'Who?'

'I may be wrong, just a feeling. A sense of another voice, a suspicion. No names, no pack drill, that's what they say, isn't it? I could be wrong. Drink up, dear.'

Charmian took another drink of loaded tea. 'This tea tastes good.' She was not going to let Winifred fall silent on this, she would come back to her.

'In certain circumstances, tea with a nip is the only drink.'

'You're right: these are certain circumstances ... You know, what you've told me, I expect you will be shocked, but I was surprised.'

Birdie had just begun to hand back the handkerchief and the scrap of paper, when her face changed. Puzzled, she turned towards Charmian. 'I believe I got it wrong ... this is the open air, there is a wind blowing and it has been raining.'

201

'Well, so it has,' said Winifred in a down to earth kind of way. 'Earlier today. Calm down, Birdie, draw it mild.' She gave her friend an anxious look. You got strokes and heart attacks that way, she had said so before.

But Birdie was going on. 'And there is blood, much blood.' Then she was violently sick.

*   *   *

Charmian walked round the corner to her own home. Muff was no longer on the tree watching, she had given up and retreated to a private sanctum of her own by the compost heap. There were mice living inside which were sometimes so unwise as to come out. Worth a cat watching. Unlike some people she had no fear of blood, the taste of which on her tongue and teeth she liked rather than otherwise. As for a severed head, she usually ate it.

The house was empty when Charmian let herself in; she expected this so she had prepared herself to cook a meal for both of them. Humphrey had promised to be back later but not too late, whatever that meant.

She changed into jeans and a shirt, put out Muff's food, and started to cook. She had got very cunning about choosing meals that were easy and quick. You lit the grill and mixed a salad, that was the way to do it.

At one time, she thought, as she peeled an onion and wiped away tears, a professional woman would have had a cook. But then, in this imagined other time, there would not have been a professional woman such as she was. She was a creature of her own time and must put up with it. Preparing thick slices of steak was not really pleasant when you had blood on your mind as a result of listening to Birdie. Flesh was flesh when all was said and done.

All was quiet outside, too dark now for the police helicopter to be surveying the ground for a hiding place. If that was what it had been doing; she had only her own speculation on that, it might just as easily have been looking for a terrorist or sorting out a traffic problem.

Probably a waste of time this afternoon with the witches. All she had done was to make poor Birdie sick. Interesting that though, because Birdie was a tough lady.

She slapped the steak hard with a rolling pin to encourage tenderness, then left it to marinade. There was some wine left over from yesterday so she poured herself a glass. Muff came in, studied her dish of food, then walked away.

'All right, be like that,' said Charmian, sipping her wine. Something ought to happen, she could feel it was time. As if to answer her, the telephone rang. She reached out a hand; if it was Humphrey saying he was going to be later after all, very late, then she was going to be angry, very angry.

But no. 'HG here. Thought you would be

interested to know that the helicopter flushed up two possible sites that are worth thinking about.'

'Are you talking about where someone could be held prisoner?'

He hesitated. 'No, not exactly ... more suggested burial places ... where a body could be. Disturbed earth and vegetation.'

'Recent?'

Again he hesitated. 'One of them. The other not so recent.'

She thought of what Birdie had said about the location of her dark, dread place. 'Near the town?'

'One of them, just on a patch of green not far from the Great Park ... The other is between Eton and Slough, nearer Slough. Too late to do anything tonight, but we will have a go tomorrow.'

'Try the nearer place first.' She owed that much to Birdie, although really neither site fitted in with what she had said. But should it? Real life and Birdie's images might not match.

'Yes.' He did not commit himself. 'Have to see what we can do. And of course, neither site might turn up anything. And the girl might walk in any minute.'

'Do you think that likely?'

'I don't know. Less and less.'

It was what Charmian thought as well. This apart, nothing matched with her own reflections or what Birdie had summoned up.

Birdie herself had produced a contradiction, of course, nothing was clear cut. But when was it ever in police work?

'It's not very easy work,' he went on gloomily. 'A real brute of a case. I felt it the minute that basement was opened up and we found what was there. And even if we locate the girl, is it going to help that investigation, which is where we started?'

'I think it might do, it's all of a piece. It's like a maze ... find the string that marks the right path through, and everything will fall into place.'

HG gave a grunt. 'You're an optimist, ma'am.'

They agreed to talk again in the morning, and Charmian went back to consider her cooking. There was no need for progress at the moment since there was no sign of Humphrey. Muff, however, had decided to eat; her head was in the bowl from which she was eating in a slow, thoughtful fashion.

'You're getting an old lady,' said Charmian, bending down to stroke her. 'I suppose we will have the dog back with us tomorrow if the witches are off.'

The thought struck her like a poisoned arrow: Birdie could not have expected Emily to turn up alive, or the two of them would have stayed at home. Missed the Laundering. Wouldn't they? Dismiss the thought, woman, she told herself. Birdie and Winifred, delightful as they are, do not have a direct line to the future. Remember that you told yourself it was a kind of wickedness, substitute silliness, to consult Birdie at all.

Muff raised her head from the dish, alerting Charmian to the sound of a car and the arrival of her husband.

'Not before time,' she said, giving him a kiss. 'Another minute and the dinner would have spoiled.'

'You haven't started to cook it.'

'Exactly what I mean: it would have been in the bin. Or Muff's dish.'

'Or the dog's. He's on his way home, I saw Winifred with him.'

'Ah, I thought he might be.' She went to the door in time to see Winifred and Benjy coming up the path.

'Off early tomorrow, so here is your boy...' Winifred handed the dog over. 'Sorry we weren't more help.'

'Maybe you will have been. How's Birdie?'

'Quite herself again. Back the day after tomorrow.' Winifred plodded back down the path to the street, then home. She looked tired.

'What did they help with?' asked Humphrey, who had been watching.

'Tell you some time. How was your day?'

'I managed to stop two representatives of NATO hitting each other, everyone hates everyone else at the moment and that's before we have the old Warsaw block countries in. I don't know what will happen there, feelings run even stronger with them. How the old Austrian-Hungarian Empire held together as long as it did, I shall never know.'

'Empires always fall apart with tears.'

'The Roman Empire didn't do too badly.'

'They got chewed up by the Goths in the end.'

'I sometimes think we are all Goths now.' But he was laughing; he was an optimist really, or he wouldn't do the work he did. The world would roll on.

They had a quiet meal, hardly talking but feeling at peace with each other. It was a good mood to be in. While she made some coffee, Charmian told him about her day, even including her session with Birdie. 'That's not for repeating, by the way.'

He could see why, but did not say so. He knew that Charmian occasionally reached out for a wilder edge on things, she had done it before.

'So now you have an identification of the dead woman in Flanders Street, and you know the child's head had been both boiled and refrigerated ... nasty that, you think the woman had been imprisoned before being killed?'

'Yes, and if so, then Emily may be in the same place.'

'But HG thinks he may have found a body?'

'I wanted him to look for a prison, but I

think he thought he ought to look for a body and he seems to have found a burial. May not be Emily. There could be another body to be found. If Rewley's strange informer was speaking the truth, then there are other human remains out there. But Rewley has not been in touch, so I can take it that the man has not surfaced either. Probably all rubbish.'

'Not like Rewley from what I have seen of him to go for rubbish.'

'Not as a rule, no.' But how steady was Rewley at the moment?

'So now you are looking for Emily, and also for Margaret Drue? And Drue, you believe, is alive and lethal.'

'That's about it.' Of course, she could always be wrong. 'The informer that spoke to Rewley said he had seen her "come out". Or words like that. So he was speaking of a woman … He could have been talking about Margaret Drue, around all the time, but in disguise.'

'And he had recognized her?'

'Yes.'

Humphrey considered. 'Coming out has come to have a special, sexual meaning.'

'She might have been bisexual.' She told him what Winifred had said.

'So she might have been going around as a man?'

Charmian nodded. 'It could be. I've been thinking that way. It would explain why she was never flushed out.'

'No wonder you are so restless.'

'Am I?' She looked down at her feet, they did look fidgety; she put them close together as if otherwise they might get away from each other. She clasped her hands firmly, fingers interlaced. No fidget there.

'Let's go for a walk. Take the dog.'

'Let's go to bed.'

'Yes, let's. Walk first, then bed.'

Charmian thought about it; she had drunk a fair amount of wine. Bed appealed, but Humphrey usually knew best. 'All right. If you say so.' She was getting to be a really dutiful wife, damn it.

Benjy was glad to take a walk, he was glad to be back with Charmian, whom he regarded both as his patron and a responsibility: you had to watch her, but she fed you well whereas the witches were trying to make a him a veggie.

Charmian wound a scarf round her head. 'Let's go to the Prince Consort Park, I like it there and Benjy can go off the lead, it's allowed there.'

They strolled off, all three in a happy mood. The night, it was right to call it night now, had turned fine with a noble moon shining on the Castle where the Royal Standard fluttered.

To reach Prince Consort Park, you left Maid of Honour Row behind you, passed the Castle Mound, and turned towards the river. You did not cross the river but turned a sharp left before the bridge. Benjy, released from his

209

leash, trotted ahead. He knew the way, one of
his best walks.

Humphrey touched Charmian's arm.
'Who's that coming towards us? It looks like
Rewley.'

'He's running,' said Charmian.

Then she stopped. 'What is he doing with his
hands? For God's sake, what is he doing with
his hands?'

CHAPTER NINE

Rewley had stopped running and was coming
towards them with a loping walk. He was
rubbing his hands over and over with what
looked like paper. Somehow that looked more
alarming to the two people watching him.

'He's wiping his hands.'

Rolling them over and over, like a hefty (he
was a big man) and unshaven Lady Macbeth.
The dog, who had been running forward,
stopped, gave a rumbling growl at the back of
his throat and stood in front of Charmian.

Her husband put a hand on her arm to hold
her back: 'Hang on a minute.'

'No, it's all right. Be quiet, dog ... It's
Rewley ... what's he doing?' And then, as he
got closer so that she could see: 'He's got blood
on him,' she said.

She moved her arm away. 'This is my job,

darling, don't protect me too much.' Benjy had retreated to sit on her feet; he didn't like what he saw any more than she did.

'When I am with you, I want to.'

Husbandly and proper, but not for me, not what I want, and I can't let you, and she moved forward. 'What is it, Rewley?' There was a lot of blood on him, on his hands and on his shirt and jeans. 'Are you all right?'

'Not my blood,' he said huskily. 'But, by God, there's a lot of it, all over the place, on the seat, on the path, on the grass, he must have bled like a pig. Alive for some time, I should think, that's why he bled so much, bled to death.'

'Who is it?' It was a man anyway, so not Emily. Did that lighten her mood? Oddly enough, not.

'My informer. I've been on the look-out for him all day, he said he'd be in the park.'

And now he was. But covered in blood and possibly dead. She looked at Rewley, who nodded.

'Yes, dead. You'd better see for yourself.' He looked down at her feet. 'Not the dog, though.'

Charmian turned to her husband: 'Call the police ... just make the usual 999 call, and they can take over. It may turn out to be something I am interested in too, but let the machine have it first ... And take the dog with you.'

'Yes, I will.' Humphrey was reluctant; he bent down to put the leash on the dog's collar.

'But I will be back. Don't go away.'

'I'll still be here. Where is the body, Rewley?'

'Up by the fountain, on one of the seats near to the water garden.'

'Right, so you know where to find me,' she said to her husband. She turned to George Rewley. 'Let's go.'

Side by side they started up the hill to the park, while Humphrey dragged Benjy away.

'So what happened? How did you come to find him?'

'I'd expected to see him earlier, any time really, but I had been keeping a look-out on the park all day in case he turned up. I thought if he was there he would wait and be looking for me. This was a last look before I gave up for the day.'

'When did you last try?'

'About eight thirty. I'd finished work for the day, that report you wanted me to do on the Morston fraud case, and I'd called in on Anny to see the child, and I went to the park on the way back. No one there. Hardly anyone about, but just enough people to make me feel he wouldn't be there ... he liked it dark and empty. That's why I tried again.'

'Do you think anyone was watching you?'

'No, I was careful. I'm sure there was no one around.'

They were at the top of the hill and looking down on the park in the moonlight.

'Someone knew where to find him, though.'

212

'He might have been followed. I don't know how he got to the park, whether he walked or had a car.'

The park gates, which were never shut now and which, like the ancient gates of Versailles at that time of the Revolution, probably could not be moved, were behind them. Ahead was the fountain, a memorial to a dead king, and beyond that the water garden. It was heavily shrouded with drooping willows.

'Yes, I can see you could be private down there ... But who was he hiding from?'

'From whoever killed him, I guess. He was frightened.'

They walked down the path. The moonlight left gentle spreading shadows into which they walked. There was a darker shadow fallen across the seat beneath the trees. They were silent as they walked towards it.

The figure lay with head hanging forward over the edge of the bench, with the torso sprawled at an angle across it, hands dangling. There was blood across the white mask, blood on the long shirt, and a pool of blood on the grass at his feet ...

'What happened to him? He didn't do this to himself, but who lets a murderer come up to him and cut his throat?'

'He was hit on the head first, I think. Then his throat was cut ... I thought his head would drop off when I lifted it.'

The shadow of Jim Towers rested on them

213

for a moment, darkening the already dark. 'Was there an attempt to cut off his head?'

'The pathologist will know more about that ... the knife cuts may show up that ... There may not have been time ... he's still warm. I may have frightened the killer off.'

'But you didn't see anyone?'

'No. I was on the way to report it when I met you.' He looked down at his hands, still bloodstained. 'I grabbed a bit of newspaper from the rubbish bin.'

'Where's your car?'

'I walked here, it seemed more discreet. I thought he might see me, follow me or know I was coming. As it turned out, he and the killer were here before me.'

'He didn't wear that mask when he went through the streets,' observed Charmian, 'whether he walked or drove. Too unpleasant.'

'Put it on as he sat down, I suppose.'

'It is a mask ... you thought it might be plaster before.'

'There is a layer of plaster on it.'

'It would certainly stop anyone sitting next to him ... This time, you had no doubt, you saw a man?'

'I know, not sure why I was confused before.'

Charmian stared down at the bloodstained figure. 'I think there is an hormonal imbalance ... the breasts are round and the hips soft ... Funny, I never noticed it before.'

Rewley said sharply: 'You know him?'

As the sound of the police patrol car arriving broke the silence, Charmian put out a hand to gently lift the mask. 'Oh yes, I know who it is, I saw him when we found the body in the basement, he was there ... It's Albert. Big Albert. He works or did work for Eddy Bell.'

Down the path hurried the heavily built police patrolman; his footsteps must have jarred the ground, because Albert rolled forward off the bench to fall, spreadeagled, face up, on the grass. He fell into the pool of blood which splashed against Charmian's foot. The blood was very fluid, she thought, how long does it take to clot?

She knelt by his side staring in his face, which was a younger face than she had remembered. But he had passed more or less unnoticed that day in the basement. Poor boy, what happened to you before or since? How did you come into possession of this lethal knowledge so that someone had to kill you? Why didn't you talk to me, not to Rewley?

There had to be a reason for that which she might know one day. There was always a reason, if you looked deep enough, for the unreasonable. She had to believe that to handle her work, and although she rarely put it into speech, it was there at the back of her mind.

Now she was close, she could see that there was a wound at the base of his head where he had been hit. He had sat on the bench, his back

215

to the trees, while he waited for Rewley. Had he sent Rewley a message to say that was where he would be? Or had he just relied on Rewley looking in the park every so often? Possibly he had watched the detective's movements earlier. If so, he had not worn the mask and general get-up. He didn't have to have it all the time, he could have hidden in the trees to dress up.

But this time there had been someone else hidden there too. The watcher had been watched. Albert's face, empty of life, was not empty of expression. He looked surprised; she had seen that look before on the victims of sudden death. She might be that way herself one day, her mouth open and her eyes wide.

She did not close Albert's eyes because that was a job for someone else, but she replaced the mask. Blood got on to her hands, but she did not move from where she sat looking at Albert. She had to say it: he made an eye-catching corpse.

She was still there when the police surgeon arrived. He was one she knew, a gentle middle-aged man called Edmunds. Dr Frank Edmunds as she remembered, and they had met before over a dead body.

He smiled at her as he deposited his black bag by her side. 'We must stop meeting this way.' He liked a joke, even if not an original one.

'Oh well, he's dead, I can say that straight off, and no doubt how it happened. Makes my

216

job easy, this sort of thing.' He was more humane than he sounded but matter of fact like all police surgeons. Must be hard on the wives, Charmian had thought. 'Come from the theatre: I'll be back in time for the last act, murder mystery, Dame Agatha.' But his hands were moving gently over the skull. 'Nasty blow there, but it didn't kill him, just rendered him ready for the knife.' He looked around. 'Got the knife?'

'I think not.'

'Well, it was sharp and thin, I'd say, and used with some force.'

'Just asking: but do you think an attempt was made to cut off the head?'

Frank Edmunds' expression did not change, he had long since lost the capacity to be startled by people like Charmian. 'Can't say. Not just by a quick look. Didn't succeed if so, didn't come near it, perhaps there wasn't time. I'm not an expert on cut off heads. I don't know if I have ever seen one.'

'They exist.'

'Haven't come my way. No, definitely not. Well, killers have strange ways, no doubt, and everyone to their taste. Must have a reason, I suppose.'

Charmian nodded. Yes, he was right, and there had to be a reason for Alana's head being cut off, and only Jim Towers was giving it attention, and, like all original thinkers, was in trouble for it. It was time she considered it

217

herself.

'A mad reason, would you think? Or a sensible reason?' Out of the corner of her eye, she could see the photographers coming down the path. She'd have to move, they both would.

'Are you asking me? Well, I suppose there's Sir Gawain and the Green Knight ... he cut off the chap's head but it grew again. And don't ask me how I know that because I am no Anglo-Saxon scholar but my daughter who's an opera buff took me to Covent Garden to see the opera. He did it because he was challenged. Great stuff.'

'I'll think about Sir Gawain,' said Charmian. She might ask Birdie for an idea if Jim Towers failed her; Birdie had been great on suggesting bloody murder close at hand. Dead right too, even to the blood in the open air. 'But meanwhile, what I am thinking is that there's a lot of blood, and it hasn't congealed. Mean anything?'

'Not as useful as a time check as we used to think. The general opinion now is that blood remains fluid in sudden death for some time. The Russians used cadaver blood in transfusions, handy on a battlefield ... In certain cases it may never coagulate. We may have one here.' He stood up, putting out a hand to help Charmian to her feet. 'Any identity?'

'He's known to me.'

'Right, well there you are ... It's up to you

218

now. You'll see my report.'

'Not really my case. It'll be for the local CID.'

He laughed. 'But you will see it, after all you were here first.'

They stood back while the scene of the crime team moved, busy in their usual tasks of taping off the ground, making measurements and taking photographs. Dr Edmunds strolled away, he never walked fast, to talk to the CID sergeant, delivering his provisional report, and Charmian went back to Rewley.

*   *   *

'So you knew him?' Rewley put the question. 'I don't know why I didn't recognize him myself.'

They were sitting on the grass where the ground rose in a gentle slope from which they could look down on the scene below. H. G. Horris had not turned up himself, he was out for the evening, but had sent one of his best watchdogs, Sergeant Samson, who was being groomed for the position Jim Towers might be losing. Charmian could have gone home, but she chose to stay for a while longer, although Sergeant Samson, a strong man with a strong name, would have been glad to see her go. Humphrey had come back but the dog had not. He sat silently beside the two of them, watching the scene below.

'No reason why. You probably never knew

him.' She reached out to a hand to touch Humphrey's. Nice of you to be here, the gesture said.

'I must have seen him: I had to go to the Bell workplace because of a break-in they had.'

'I didn't know about that.'

'It was some time ago, before I was working full-time for you ... I was seconded to Ron Fraser's team for a few months. The break-in was a small-time affair. Bell didn't seem worried, I don't think he would have reported it if a neighbour hadn't seen the lad running away and got on the blower for him ... Bell was more interested in the new outhouse he was building for Dr Yeldon as far as I could tell.'

'Did you get anyone for the robbery?'

'Oh, it was one of the Cheasey boys, one of the Elderberry lot, serving his apprenticeship to the local Mafia; he was easily identified, left his fingerprints all over the place, he won't go far in the trade, I remember thinking. But Eddy wouldn't prosecute.'

'Good of him.'

'Just didn't want to bother. But his father had just died, so it may have been that. Not that it did the boy a lot of good, he fell under a car a year later and goes round in a wheelchair. I reckon that one of his own lot did it to him, you know how ruthless they are, even with their own, if they get let down, and the boy showed all the signs of being a non-achiever. Anyway, that was when I must surely have seen

Albert, passed him in the yard at least.'

'It explains how he knew you, that's one question answered.'

'Doesn't explain why he went around dressed up like a guy.'

'It does if he was frightened, scared silly. And it looks as though he was right to be frightened.'

Rewley admitted it. 'True enough.'

'What was it he said: I saw her come out? So what did he mean? I'm guessing that he meant Margaret Drue . . . that she has been around all the time. Wearing a man's dress. And that he recognized her. Either she "came out" as he put it, or gave herself away in some manner.'

'Are you suggesting that she killed him?'

'Yes, it's what I am thinking. It has to be so, doesn't it?'

'Then where has she been hiding? And where is she now?'

'We'll find her, don't worry about that. We'll get her in the end, whatever face she has put on.' She got to her feet, Sergeant Samson was coming her way. Chucking out time had come.

The moon had gone behind a bank of clouds, it was no longer a pleasant night, but in spite of this and the lateness of the hour, a small group of onlookers had arrived to see what was going on. The stringer from the local paper had turned up; he recognized Charmian, so he was moving quietly in her direction with the thought that if he was lucky he would get there before Sergeant Samson. He knew Samson too, and would name him in his piece; he got his facts right, with plenty of detail which he knew made for a good sale. He might risk a photograph too, he had his small camera under his arm.

He was not lucky, the Sergeant got to Charmian first. 'Just packing up, ma'am. Getting the site under cover in case of rain, with a chap on duty to keep an eye on it. We'll be back tomorrow to carry on. Can't really do much with the light as it is.'

Even assisted by the lamps that had been rigged up with power from a police van, it was too murky under the bushes and trees for a proper search.

'Anything useful?' Charmian asked.

'No knife,' said Samson. 'The doc said it would be a small, sharp piece, so it would be easy to carry away. The perp' would get blood on his clothes, but he probably had that anyway. Someone might have noticed. We'll be asking.'

'Anything else?'

'A branch from a tree the size of a baseball bat with blood on it,' he said reluctantly. 'Have to check it, of course.'

'That's interesting ... Makes it look as if the killer came with the knife all ready to use, but used something on the spot for the blow on the head. Half premeditated and half spontaneous.'

222

'I think it was planned all right, the knife would have to have been ready and sharp...'

'Yes.' Birdie had been right about the blood in the open, she hadn't mentioned a knife. Perhaps the darkness she had seen at first had been under the trees.

'We will go over the ground thoroughly tomorrow ... I've spoken to Superintendent Horris, ma'am, and he would be glad to have a talk with you tomorrow ... You identified the victim.'

'Yes, I did. And I'd like to talk to him. Get him to ring me.' It would do no harm to remind the Sergeant, and through him, HG, of her superior rank. She didn't expect a bow from Samson, nor did she get one, but she got a grin.

'Right, ma'am, will do.' He considered saluting but thought better of it, you could go so far with ma'am but no further. He was a judicious man as well as ambitious.

The three of them walked out of the park and down the hill, enjoying the movement and the night air; the moon was out again in a clear sky.

'He nearly saluted you as we left,' said Humphrey.

'He knew better...' She turned to Rewley. 'Don't go back to the flat tonight. Stay with us, there's plenty of room.'

Rewley didn't need any persuading, he hated his empty home. 'Thank you.'

She left the two men together, talking, while

she went to make up the bed. When she came back with a tray of coffee and sandwiches, they were deep in a discussion. 'I thought you might be hungry.' It was obvious to her that Rewley was not eating much lately. Fine, it was part of grieving, possibly a necessary part, but there were limits.

She was pleased when he took a sandwich with a murmur of thanks. Then he turned to her. 'Humphrey thinks you've got it wrong.'

'Does he?' She raised an eyebrow. Her husband did not usually pass a comment on her work. It worked both ways: she left him alone.

'Yes, about Margaret Drue, I think you are wrong there.'

Charmian took a sandwich, which she did not really want, to chew while she thought about it. 'You think she's not there?'

'Oh yes, she's there. But perhaps you are getting it wrong. You are too obsessed with her.'

Charmian swallowed her mouthful, and began to sum up. 'Look, when we found the body and the child's head, where I came into the case really because my name was there, on the body, it was concluded that it was Drue, and she had been killed in a revenge killing by someone close to the child.'

'A wrong identification, as it turned out.'

'Yes, I admit, all of us jumped to the wrong conclusion there. The dead woman was

Madelaine Mason. We don't know why she was killed but she could have recognized Drue in whatever guise she was going round and been killed. I don't know the motive for her death, perhaps she tried some blackmail, but she was killed. I think she was imprisoned, knew she was about to be killed and tried to get out a message for help.'

'So once again, you tried out Drue for size?'

'Yes, I did, and I felt as though she fitted. I still feel that way. I think Emily knew Drue was around, possibly she recognized her, and let Drue see it. I think she is imprisoned in the way Mason was. I don't know where the blood in Emily's room came from, perhaps it was Drue, I'd like to think of her bleeding.'

'There's a lot of guesswork there.'

Charmian bit into the sandwich again, she was feeling hungry now, as she defended herself. 'Try guessing better.'

'I think you are obsessed with her.'

'Well, maybe. I suspected Jim Towers at one point, if we are talking about obsessions.'

Humphrey spoke up with decision. 'No, it's too complicated. She could never have done all that.'

'I didn't say she did it alone,' said Charmian slowly. 'She may have had help.'

'And about Towers ... there you go again. He's just an unhappy chap who's at odds with his wife and perhaps more in love with Dolly than she is with him.'

'She is in love with him,' said Charmian.

Rewley stopped eating. 'No, not Dolly, she's sorry for him, that's all. You know what she's like. She can't see a lame dog without picking it up and carrying it along.'

Charmian felt tired and beleaguered: they were not helping her. 'Listen, have you forgotten where we were tonight? Albert has been killed, slaughtered, that's the way it looks to me. He was at the school when we found the body and the child's head, he had known the school and the family for years because he was at the same school as Emily and Eddy Bell, he must have known the Drue woman. Known what she looked like, anyway. He was terrified, so much so that he tried to mask himself.' She swung round to face Rewley, 'And he said to you that he saw her come out ... I think he recognized Drue, that she knew it, and killed him.'

She thought she had silenced them both, until she saw that Rewley had dropped asleep in the chair.

She got up. 'I'm going to bed,' she said to her husband. 'You wake him up and see he gets there too.'

She climbed the stairs to her room; she was glad to leave both men behind her. No doubt in the morning she would be glad to see them again, but now she needed to be on her own. She felt exhausted, she was tired all over, her body ached, and her mind felt emptied.

Muff was asleep on the bed, already stowed away for the night. Charmian patted her plump curving back as she threw off her clothes to prepare for a shower; it seemed necessary to wipe the night away. Everything she had removed she threw into the basket ready to be washed. There was no blood on her clothes but she felt stained.

They were right, those two downstairs, she was taking it too personally. Obsessed? She wouldn't accept that notion though, a little trace of male chauvinism there. Let them talk about obsession, they had the odd traces themselves. Humphrey was mildly obsessive about his country house, and Rewley, well he was certainly obsessed with his child at the moment, but one couldn't blame him for that.

She stood under the shower, letting the hot water play on her back, not blaming anyone and feeling gently benevolent. It was an old-fashioned bathroom which she had not done much to when she moved in, beyond repainting it and installing a shower cabinet at one end. The basin and bath had brass taps which had to be polished and the bath stood four-square on rounded legs; it was a comfortable, homely room in which you felt safe. In Charmian's life, safety was a precious possession to be valued.

It was a bathroom which demanded thick, soft white towels and a maid to polish the taps. Since she did not have a maid, she polished the taps herself. Sometimes. As she wrapped the

227

towels round herself she could see that some time had been a long time ago. You could probably train a husband to polish brass taps.

A cat you could not train, she thought, going back into the bedroom. She looked down at Muff, sleeping peacefully. 'There is one thing I have forgotten, cat,' she said aloud, 'and that is what Albert said to Rewley, and I quote as told to me, that "there were other human remains". And he was not talking about himself.'

She stood there thinking: H. G. Horris had two sites of possible buryings she hoped he would get on and investigate them.

*　　　*　　　*

She awoke to the smell of frying bacon, not a smell often met with in that house, and someone whistling. The bed beside her was empty, but had been slept in, the cat had gone too. From the bathroom was the sound of water running.

She put on her dressing-gown, avoided Muff who met her on the stairs, and went into the kitchen. Rewley was standing at the stove, turning bacon in the pan with a fork and whistling. Not a tune she could recognize, possibly no tune at all, just a cheerful sound.

'How are you this morning? Did you sleep well?'

'I feel fine, better than for a long while. I think I had that chap on my mind, and now

228

he's appeared, I feel better. A weight off my shoulders.'

'Even if he is dead?'

'Yes, terrible isn't it? No accounting for the human mind ... I shall call on Anny this morning and make some strong noises about the child, she's had it all her own way long enough.'

'I won't argue with that.'

'I thought you wouldn't mind me cooking some breakfast. Can I do you some?'

'Make me some coffee. No bacon for me, though.'

She went upstairs, where her husband was just emerging from the bathroom.

'You seem to have cured Rewley,' she said to him.

'He did it himself.'

'Did you stay up all night?'

'A fair amount of it.'

She had dressed in a skirt and a silk shirt, it was going to be that sort of day, definitely not one for jeans. 'And what did you talk about?'

'That's private between him and me.'

She accepted this in a peaceable fashion. 'All right, I won't take offence. It seems to have worked, he's down there eating, and what's more, you can go into the kitchen and eat with him.'

'Is that a threat?'

'I think I would call it an ultimatum, wouldn't you?'

She left him upstairs and went down to claim her cup of coffee. 'You make a good cup,' she said.

'Kate taught me.' He was beginning to be able to talk about Kate again, he had spent most of the night telling Humphrey about her and how he felt. The pain had eased. He had been so surrounded by women, kind, helpful women, but he realized now that there were times you needed your own sex. 'Not a natural skill of mine, I used to buy the powder and put it in a mug, now I do the thing properly.'

'Kate instructed me too ... it was after she came back from Italy.' Then she stopped talking, because Kate had gone to Italy with a man who was not Rewley.

'It's all right ... I know all about that, Kate and I had it out ages ago, and after all I didn't know her then. I had my own confessions to make, and perhaps I did not tell her every detail nor she to me. But she did hand over the coffee machine, and I guess she gave you yours too...' He looked at the shining glass and chrome apparatus on the table.

'She did.'

Charmian got up. 'I must go now. It's going to be a difficult day.' She could hear Humphrey coming down the stairs, and from the sound of it, the cat as well. 'Cook some more bacon, will you? They will both want some.'

She called a goodbye up the stairs with a promise to telephone, and departed. Her car

230

started with no fuss, which was a good sign.

H. G. Horris was on the telephone as soon as she was sitting at her desk, he might have spies on her. His voice was gruff, his bad-day voice. 'So you've got another one for me.' He could be a very aggressive man, but the thing was not to let him know you had noticed.

'Is it one for you then?'

'Since it's Albert Batting, who worked for Eddy Bell and was there when the body and head was found, yes, I think it is.'

'I suppose you interviewed him then?'

'We did and got nothing. Claimed to have seen nothing much and known less ... just went along in the day's work ... Maybe did know nothing about that business but he must have known something about something.'

'You'll have to dig deeper.'

'Oh we will, don't worry. Friends, enemies, contacts ... trouble is, I don't think he had many. Lived on his own in the cottage where he had lived with his mother. It's run-down and neglected but he was a sitting tenant and couldn't be turned out. Not that anyone wanted to, as far as I can find out ... he had his odd little ways, like not washing too much, but he was thought to be harmless.'

'What about his employer?'

'Eddy Bell? Gives him a good record. Always came to work on time, even these last few days, and did a good day's work. Not bright, but willing.'

231

What an epitaph, Charmian thought.

'There must be more,' HG went on, 'but we will have to find it. The girl Emily might be a help if we can find her.'

And if she is alive, he did not add, but Charmian thought. 'No news of her, I suppose?'

'You would have had it, ma'am.'

I stand corrected, Charmian thought, put in my place. Of course, I would have had it.

'I suppose today you will be looking at the sites the helicopter identified as recent buryings?' She had asked him to look for the prison for a live girl, but he had chosen to look for a grave. Perhaps he was right. 'Go for the nearer one first.'

'You have information?'

'No, just a feeling.' How could you say that a witch had said that the 'dark, black place' was near at hand? And if she had simply been reading Charmian's own imagination, what was the point?

'I'll do my bit, ma'am.'

There it was again, the sharp reminder that he knew her rank was above his. He really was a cagey, sour devil. But clever and wily and honest.

Jumped up cow, thought HG. Over-promoted, pushed into high office, given powers I don't know all about. He did know, or guessed as they all did, that part of her job was secret. That she checked on more than he knew of, and had contacts in powerful places. What took her to that committee in Knightsbridge so regularly? Ask questions and you get no answers.

Now married to someone who was the same only more so. Even higher rank in an unspecified office. Not that he suspected her of marrying for this reason. He'd seen them together more than once and it was not only a marriage of mind and common interest. No, sex came into it. Well, good luck to her.

He did not truly resent her, or dislike her in any personal way, she was a good-looking woman with a nice voice; his anger was routine and would have been levelled at any woman with more power than he had. Nor was he alone in this, his reaction was shared by more than half the force. In his age group, anyway. Perhaps the younger ones were different. She was honest though, and straightforward, even if she phrased her words carefully, and HG acknowledged this as a virtue.

Phrasing her words carefully, Charmian said: 'I'll be in London for part of the day, but back by late afternoon.'

'We'll be looking for the knife ... But it won't be there.'

'No?'

'No, from what the police surgeon and now forensics say it was a special bit of steel, a knife of quality, and a knife like that has a pedigree that might be traceable. No, you don't leave a knife like that lying around: he's got it with him.'

'I think you are right.'

It was the sort of point on which HG could be relied upon to be right.

'Where is the first site you are digging?'

'Bridge Hill, by the old railway cutting, where the line went through Cheasey to Slough and then Paddington before the line was closed.'

'I know it.' A bitter, malodorous place where more than one body could be buried by the feel of it. 'I'd come if I hadn't got an urgent appointment. And the other place?'

'Edge of the Great Park, this side, near Egham.'

'Ah. Further away.' And more salubrious. Not far from Runnymede, where King John met the Barons and sealed the Charter. A better spot to lie buried altogether, and if the river rose high and the ground flooded, as well it might, probably safer for the killer. But quite an open spot, you'd have to be cunning to avoid being seen doing your spot of burying.

'A bit public too.' Unlike the gloomy recesses of the old railway line.

'Yes, you'd need to be handy with your transport and your spade.'

'I'll phone you when I get back.'

'Or I will see you get a message.'

There it was again: the not too delicate hint not to interfere. But no one had ever said that

234

HG was delicate. Certainly no one who had lived or worked with him.

She had a long, and it had to be admitted, somewhat acrimonious day in London, so much so that she would have been glad to be back in Windsor if it had not been such a murderous spot. She had managed to telephone her husband very briefly. It had been a pleasure to hear a quiet, friendly voice, and their conversation had been for the most part private and personal, until the end.

'And you spoke to your Superintendent?'

'He's not my Superintendent. I have my own little team, but he isn't on it.'

'And did you tell him to look for Margaret Drue?'

'It's hard to tell him anything. But I felt tempted to tell him to look for a well-built woman who might be dressed as a man. Only I didn't. Might have been counter-productive, the way he is. All the same,' she paused, 'I think he is looking. Only for a burial at the moment.'

Then they went back to personal chat.

She got back to her office in time to receive a message from the Superintendent. It was on her answerphone but it had only just come in.

'It was a donkey.'

There was no request to telephone the Incident Room, or rooms since more than one linked investigation was going on, but she did so nevertheless. HG answered her at once, he must have been expecting her call.

'Tell me about the donkey.'

She could hear the gust of his sigh over the line: 'An aged beast, left over from the last fair here. A natural death from age. Buried tenderly with his bridle, so someone loved him. Not long dead, but a dead donkey.'

'Reburied now, I suppose?'

'The public health people say he shouldn't be there, so I suppose he was tucked away there one dark night, about two weeks ago it would be, by someone who didn't want to send him to the knackers' or the town tip.'

'And tomorrow?' she queried.

'Yes, tomorrow we shall start digging again, at the other site. Too late today and one dead donkey a day is enough.'

'I'd like to come. If I may?'

He knew she would be there, and the only way was to be gracious. 'I'll send a car,' and then he paused, 'ma'am.'

Charmian grinned as she put the telephone down. She knew how he felt.

It was evening but there was shopping to be done. Food shopping. Even Charmian, undomestic as she claimed to be, was the one who bought the food which fed her household. In fact, she enjoyed doing it. She looked at her watch: time enough, all the shops she dealt with stayed open until late several nights a week of which this was one.

She parked her car in the large car park of her favourite store and selected a trolley. She

236

wondered whom she would meet tonight of her friends and neighbours. One of the pleasures of this shopping was that she met people she was glad to see and only seemed to meet in the shops. All as busy as she was, she supposed.

The town had seemed quiet as she had driven through it from Maid of Honour Row, but she knew there would be policemen all over the town, asking questions about where Emily had been seen, and where she might be. Also about Albert ... Poor Albert who had lived alone in his untidy home; she had read the first report before she came out shopping and it was already clear that there would be few to mourn him.

'Neighbours say they hardly ever saw him, that he never touched the garden, which is knee-high in weeds and muck, and the dustbin stayed unemptied till they complained. On hygiene grounds, they won't miss him. Personally either, as he never spoke. They don't know what he lived on, but judging by what they saw falling out of the bin it was curry or fish and chips.'

He didn't shop here then, thought Charmian, as she pushed her trolley down the aisle with fruit on one side and vegetables on the other.

'There is a dog, white and brown mongrel bitch,' the report had gone on. 'Now in the police pound.'

What had he fed the dog on then? Chicken

curry and poppadoms?

She grabbed several varieties of lettuce, some avocados and a cucumber from one side, veered across the aisle to collect apples and pears.

'Hi,' said a protesting voice, 'that was my toe ... Oh sorry, Miss Daniels, didn't see it was you.' It was one of the girls from the large typing pool in the main police building; they knew each other by sight.

'Sorry, my fault.' Charmian apologized. 'Thinking of other things.' Like fillet steak, which she didn't much like but husbands seemed to, French bread, and butter not butter substitute. Soap and washing powder, not bio because Mrs Grady who did the laundry did not care for it. 'Brings me up in a rash.'

She had to make her way to all these things. She could see Dolly's head down the aisle, past the bread display, choosing biscuits. That probably meant she still had Jim Towers staying with her as Dolly was always on a strict diet which forbade biscuits.

No sign of Birdie and Winifred, not to be expected, even if they were back from the Laundering trip; they shopped in various specialist stores concentrating on healthy organic food loaded with vitamins. Even Benjy ate like that when he stayed with them and only Muff the cat stayed loyal to fish and meat.

She waved to Dolly, who waved back before returning with an abstracted air to the biscuit selection.

There was Dr Yeldon and his wife; Dr Yeldon was pushing the trolley and his wife appeared to be pushing him. She fancied it was usually that way round.

They seemed to be meeting friends on every side because she could see smiles and greetings as they went round the aisles.

She finished her shopping as quickly as she could, then surveyed the checkout desks for the one with the shortest line-up of shoppers. She found herself joined by the Yeldons, whose trolley was, she observed with interest, well loaded with bottles of wine and whisky. Who'd have thought it?

Were they embarrassed to meet her and let her see their purchases? Dr Yeldon looked a bit shifty but his wife smiled, her large, yellow teeth clear and bold.

'Nice to see a friend,' said Mrs Yeldon. Dr Yeldon smiled and muttered something about the necessity for friends to keep in touch, which did not make sense to Charmian who had not guessed she was a friend, or not that sort. Not drunk already, she thought, no surely not.

His wife was certainly not drunk or under the weather of any sort, her smile, although broad and unwavering, was arctic cold. Not sure if I want to be a friend to that smile, Charmian thought, but perhaps you could not choose your friends but had to take what the gods offered. Did a lifetime of friendship with

Mrs Yeldon stretch ahead of her?

She caught up with Dolly Barstow in the car park where she was glad to see that Dolly had bought things other than biscuits. Plenty of them though, chocolate and plain, also swiss rolls, fruit cake and currant buns.

'Having a tea-party for Baby and assorted nannies,' she explained, noticing Charmian's observing gaze. 'The kid is my godchild ... Anny is coming and so is Rewley. Do you want to come? Saturday, the only day that suits them all.'

'I might look in.' Charmian was cautious, it might be better to leave them alone to see what happened. Several cars away, she could see Mrs Yeldon preparing to drive off, with Dr Yeldon in the car beside her like another bundle. 'Not thinking of asking the Yeldons?'

Dolly raised an eyebrow. 'You must be joking. She's poison that woman, my spies tell me that she's sent him in practically daily asking about progress in the investigation. I don't know how he bears it.'

'With the help of the bottle, I think,' said Charmian. 'But takes a keen interest himself, I seem to remember.'

'I don't like civilians to be so keen.' Dolly was sharp. 'They ought to stay out of it. I always suspect their motives.'

'I suppose those two were fond of the Bailey family.'

'Oh well, maybe.'

240

'And right to be worried about Emily...'

'No news of her?'

Charmian shook her head. Why mention a grave due to be dug in the morning?

* * *

In the morning, she was ready for the car when it came. Not ready for the grave, which she found stomach-turning in a way she had never expected.

The dig had begun long before she arrived; she knew as soon as she approached the site that there was something wrong with this grave. For one thing, it was old, too old. Not immemorially old, not the burial place of a Roman, or a Saxon, both of whom might have lived and died and been buried in Egham, but too old to be the grave of Emily.

Yet there was a body in it; as diggers got further down, they moved the soil with great delicacy. All around on the ground above the dig, the piled up earth was being sieved by other men. It might contain clues. But so far nothing had shown up except the bones of a small animal.

As a foot appeared, sticking up at an angle, the diggers stopped and looked up at HG.

'Yes, go on, but use your hands.'

He turned to Charmian. 'It's coming, whatever is there, it's coming up. About time too, I feel as though I've been here all day already.' He had shaved early so that a thin dark line was already showing on his upper lip; he had had a moustache in early youth before joining the force, and the ghost of it hung around.

'That is a woman's shoe,' said Charmian. A court shoe with a high heel, probably light brown in colour once, but now stained with earth and blotched with what might be blood.

'Make a guess who it is?'

'Won't try,' Charmian answered, her eyes on the legs which were now appearing; one leg was bent against the body and it was on this leg that they could see the shoe. The other leg lay straight but was shoeless. Not much trouble seemed to have been taken in burying this body: a hole had been made and the body dropped in it. The earth had covered it and grass and weeds had grown over the top. Except for the miracle of the modern camera with its trick of seeing into the earth, it might never have been discovered.

Not true, Charmian thought while she watched; this discovery is at the end of a chain which began when Nancy Bailey died and the heirs in Australia decided the house in Windsor must be sold. Thus Emily had been obliged to uncover the basement room and reveal what was inside. Then she had disappeared, and Albert had been killed. She was probably dead herself, but she was not here, in this grave.

A length of muddied pleated skirt appeared,

still attached to the body and covering the rib cage, pelvis and upper legs. What colour it had been was doubtful, it had melted into the earth and been tinged with earth colours. The colour could be revived in the laboratory, but something about the stripes reminded her of the summer when the soft striped skirt was all the rage. She had worn one herself. Her skirt had been blue and white; popular colours had been a strong yellow and a mild orange, this one might have been yellow.

The skull shone white, the flesh fallen away, although a little seemed to hang on the cheekbones and on the jaw. A fall of dark hair still on it, straggling like underground vegetation.

She looked at HG. 'I guess now.'

It was like one of those games where you are given three guesses. Or a fairy story where the traveller or the princess is allowed three guesses.

I guess this is a woman. Because of the shoes. I guess this is not a young woman, but a woman of a certain age, because of those shoes which are old in style, dark court shoes, not the shoes of a young woman. I guess she has been dead for about ten years, because skirts of the sort she seems to have been wearing … it is badly torn, I observe … were fashionable about that length of time ago.

Apparently, she had said all this aloud. There was a silence while HG considered her

243

words. 'That's three guesses.'

'Did I say that aloud? Well, I'm not ashamed.'

'Have another go,' said HG, turning his back on the grave and walking away. 'We all will.'

I guess what we have found is the body of Margaret Drue.

CHAPTER TEN

'So there we are,' said HG.

'It is Margaret Drue,' said Charmian with conviction and a sense of shock.

'I think so too.' The Superintendent looked as solid as ever, his body swelled out by the exertions of his morning, but his face was troubled, and sad. Not really an emotion she associated with HG.

Sad? Charmian observed his face again. Surely not sad about a woman whom he had not known and whose history he had disliked? No, not sad for her, but sad because his prime suspect for several murders was now seen to have been dead herself for years. Yes, she couldn't blame him for a pang over that, bad luck, HG, she thought. Case down the drain.

But perhaps Drue had been the first killer, the murderer of the child, and possibly also of Madelaine Mason? Then killed herself by a revengeful unknown figure? That was the scenario with which they had started after all. Could they go back to it?

But no, even as she thought about it, Charmian found the idea carried less and less conviction this time round. She couldn't accept it. It had never been a very good idea, just an optimistic one, that this would turn out to be a case already solved. But some mysteries were never solved, it might be that this was going to be one of them.

She joined HG in a fit of sadness. A passing mood of sadness which she suppressed with a quick hand, first because she did not wish to join HG in any mood, and also because it was such a second-class emotion in the circumstances. She was going to flush out this killer, she was determined on it. And now the false theory of Margaret Drue was out of the way, it might be easier.

Ideas were already beginning to form in her mind.

In HG's, it seemed they were not. He looked empty of ideas. He rarely had ideas, he was a routine man, who worked away doggedly until the truth came up and hit him like a brick wall.

'What we've got to do now,' Charmian said, 'is to find Emily.'

'Have been trying,' he said heavily. 'Not much to go on, the blood didn't help. According to Dr Yeldon, who was her doctor, it was her blood type, but common enough.'

'So she is wounded? Might be dead by now. Dead or alive, in one piece or bits, we want her.'

HG looked at her with heavy sadness; what a horrible way of putting things she had, this woman, whose intellect he respected, whose career he had to admire, but who got up his nose. He hated coppers in skirts.

'Only guessing.' Another thing he hated was having to guess. Gloomily he added: 'Have to call in another pathologist. The queue of bodies is getting too long.' He was aware of almost having made a joke. 'Our chap is too busy.'

'Try Hedda Robinson from Reading,' said Charmian. 'She's brilliant. Young too.'

Lovely, thought HG, just what I wanted. But he was aware he would follow Charmian's advice and that he would be wise to do so: she gave good advice.

'I'd better get back,' said Charmian. 'Thank you for letting me come. I'm glad I did. I wanted to see for myself.'

HG led her towards the car that had brought her out to the site where the police crews were already at work. The body would be photographed, studied in detail on the spot, then taken away in a plain van. The media had not arrived yet, but the word would get round.

'I'll have to stay.' He saw Charmian to the car, holding the door politely. 'See things set up here, then I'll be off back myself. Not much I

246

can do here.'

And frankly, not much I can do back in my office, except read reports on Albert, on Madelaine Mason and on the child's head. They don't tell me much. Plenty of questions asked by a number of diligent officers, but there seem to be no witnesses and no one with much to say.

On the road overlooking the digging area, several pressmen had already arrived. H. G. Horris dealt with them briskly and briefly. 'No, nothing to say yet, I will be holding a press conference later. Yes, you will be told when and where.' But they were both photographed.

Driving back into Windsor towards her office, Charmian let her thoughts roam. Ideas were flitting in and out, she did not dwell on one particular notion yet, but it felt good. She was beginning to see a pattern of events.

But where to go? She needed Emily, dead or alive. She still thought that the girl was alive and shut up somewhere. No good going to the witches again; all that had come from that mad experiment had been talk of darkness and death, and although it had happened to have a certain relevance to events as they turned out later, Birdie's visions had not produced Emily. Come close, she was beginning to think, but not done the job.

Back in her office, she had the day's bundle of work and messages to deal with, and while her mind operated on these with its usual smoothness, underneath thoughts about Emily were rumbling away. She had asked H. G. Horris whom he had questioned about the girl, which friends and neighbours had been asked for details, for anything that could give a clue to what could have happened to her.

'Had the lot questioned,' he had answered. 'Not that it amounted to much in the end: girls she worked with, people in the same group in that course she was doing...' he was cavalier in the way he described Emily's studies, of which he obviously thought little. 'They had nothing much of use, she was friendly but not communicative, or not to them. If she had closer friends to whom she did talk, I haven't found them. She was a loner.' He was one himself, in a way, so this at least was something he understood. 'So I went back to the people from the school to see what they remembered: Dr Yeldon and his missus, the old gardener... I even had a word with Jim Towers.'

'What did he have to say?' she had asked.

'Nothing much, says she was never there as a child, and that he knows nothing of her as a girl now, except what we all know, what you know, ma'am.'

But you don't believe him, she had thought, and what that means, I don't know.

'It's all there in the reports which you get,' HG had said.

And it was. She put her hand on the reports where they sat on her desk. What she had there

248

was all the information that had been brought in by all the officers, put on file, and written up. It didn't make for exciting reading.

She listened to Dr Yeldon's tape again, she had already done so once. Talk, a laugh.

She sat thinking; she drank more of the coffee in the pot on the hot-plate, left ready for her. It had been there all day so it tasted stewed and thick, but it seemed to work. She could feel ideas, or one idea, emerging. Sensational, horrible, but something to hang on to.

It had all started when the wall went down. Before that, years and years of silence. Several dead bodies stowed away, but silence. Quiet. Then things started to happen.

Albert knew something and was killed. Emily knew something. She disappeared, and we can't get a hold on where she is or why. No one seems to know much. That silence is still operating.

She drank some black coffee and let the thoughts assemble themselves. The pattern they began to make was not agreeable, but she needed something solid to hang it upon. Like a picture on a wall, it needed a peg. She remembered a laugh, and wondered.

A thought scrambled up from the depths. What about going to Dr Yeldon? He was very anxious about the whole business, held his 'street party', went to check on where Emily lived when he heard there might be trouble. Trouble, she thought, that's an
249

understatement for this nightmare. But he might know more than we've got out of him so far.

He had not laughed, but the evidence of the tape suggested that someone had done. She picked up the telephone to speak to the Superintendent. 'Would it be true to say that you are pulling out everything to find Emily?'

He was silent for a moment while she willed him to say what she wanted. Then, his voice husky, he said: 'I'll turn Windsor over stone by stone, if I have to.'

Charmian laughed. 'That's what I wanted to hear. Can I quote you?'

*   *   *

The Yeldons' house was older and greyer than she had expected, heavy, substantial grey stone and well over a hundred years old. The front garden had a lawn and shrubbery but not many flowers. Dr Yeldon was in the garden when she called, pruning a bush (was it really the season of the year for pruning roses?) and looking as if the greyness and the heaviness of his house weighed him down. He was a large man who had gone hollow inside with age. His face suggested he might be sick. And if so, with what illness? Even doctors could fail to diagnose their own ills. Or might not want to, if the prognosis was bad. Be gentle with this man, she told herself, he may need you to be.

Mrs Yeldon appeared through the side garden gate, her expression watchful. Whatever he's got, she knows, Charmian decided. She's guarding him, protecting him. You did protect your own property, didn't you, and he was valuable to her. He represented a big expenditure of her time and energy—her life in short, and you couldn't get more valuable than that. Goodness knows why he needed protection, perhaps Mrs Yeldon thought all men did.

Dr Yeldon stood up when he saw Charmian. He looked surprised. 'You've got news? About Emily?' Without waiting for an answer, he advanced towards her. 'We've heard about Albert, of course. Poor fellow, poor boy. Not one of the brightest and easily led, but with a good heart.'

'One of your patients?'

'His parents were, they are long dead, but I didn't see much of Albert. Never ill, splendid specimen physically but not too much up above.' He was still carrying a small garden fork. 'The firm he worked for have been putting up a new garden shed for us.' He looked over his shoulder. 'In the back garden. All done now, so we haven't seen the lad nor expected to, it was a considerable shock, though.' Then he added gravely, 'Anything about Emily?'

'No, sorry.'

Dr Yeldon shook his head. 'A bad business,

however way you look it. The investigation going slowly, eh? Perhaps I shouldn't ask, one knows these things have to be confidential.'

'The death of Albert opens things up, don't you think?'

Dr Yeldon put on his spectacles as if this would help him see things more clearly.

'He and Emily knew each other,' went on Charmian. 'There has to be a connection.'

Mrs Yeldon came up to where Charmian still stood, holding the gate open. 'Do come in, dear. Is there anything we can do?'

They had not heard about the finding of Margaret Drue's body, nor did she intend to tell them, H. G. Horris would be making his own announcement there.

'I know you two were concerned about Emily, that the whole business worried you, and you probably know more about the background to the death of the child Alana and Madelaine Mason...'

Dr Yeldon pursed his lips. 'We told the police all we knew, at the time, didn't we, my dear?' He looked at his wife, who nodded. 'And really it wasn't so much, it seemed a happy little school and Nancy was a nice woman. My wife knew her better than I did.'

'No one really knew Nancy well,' said Mrs Yeldon.

'So I gathered.'

'I don't think we can add to those earlier statements.'

'Wish we could,' put in her husband.

'And what about friends and neighbours who came to what you called your street party?'

'They have been questioned, but I don't know what they added. Their part was really general concern for a terrible crime, but they were in no sense involved. Not even as much we were.'

'Not involved,' said Mrs Yeldon, putting her hand on her husband's shoulder.

'Only as friends, my dear, and that did involve us ... no man is an island and all that sort of thing.'

'Oh, you are too good for your own good,' said his wife, letting her arm fall away as if she did not quite mean it. There was irritation in her voice. 'Are you coming in, my dear?'

'No, just let me know if anything comes to mind.'

'Such as?'

'Anything from the past that strikes you, anything about Emily now. Anything your friends might tell you ... they may say something to you that they would not tell the police ... Just let me know.'

Mrs Yeldon looked thoughtful. 'If you say so.'

'And I want you to be sure that the police are really pulling out all the stops to find Emily ... wherever she is. The Superintendent says he will pull Windsor down stone by stone if he has to.'

'I don't think the Queen would like that,' said Mrs Yeldon. 'But I am glad he is really trying, we did begin to wonder how seriously he took her absence.'

'Oh very seriously. Very seriously. She is the key to everything.'

'Do you think so?'

'Yes,' Charmian assured her. 'Once Albert was found, Emily's position came into perspective. They knew each other, those two. Albert had something he wanted to say.'

The two Yeldons nodded their heads together at the same moment.

'Emily has to be found, then she can tell us what she knows.'

'Do you mean she is hiding so that she cannot tell?'

'Well, it has to be thought about.'

'You are not saying she killed Albert? Oh surely not?'

Charmian said: 'As to that, I cannot know yet, but she has knowledge.'

'What about the blood, her blood?'

'It is easy to spill blood,' said Charmian. 'She may have cut herself, or someone may have done it to her...'

'What is it you are trying to say, Miss Daniels?'

'Would you protect her, Dr Yeldon?'

'No, certainly not, not beyond a point.'

'Have you reached that point?'

'I have no idea where the girl Emily is,' he said solemnly. 'You must believe me.'

'I do believe you,' said Charmian. 'I just wanted to be sure ... in that case, Emily is either dead or imprisoned.'

Dr Yeldon put away his spectacles, he no longer wished to see too clearly. 'That is a horrible idea.'

'Yes,' said Charmian, 'which is why we must all help the police find her ... Will you speak to your friends? See what they know.'

'Nothing,' said Mrs Yeldon. 'How could they?'

'But someone does, someone, somewhere, knows everything.'

Dr Yeldon began to shake. 'Would you like a cup of tea, Miss Daniels, your ladyship, I mean?'

'Miss Daniels will do,' said Charmian, her voice unpromising.

The shakes grew worse. 'I think I will have one, yes, a nice hot cup of tea.'

His wife touched his arm. 'You go in, I will follow.' She watched her husband as he shuffled off, hanging on to the wall as he passed. Then she turned to Charmian. 'What was all that about?'

Charmian was silent for a moment, framing her words carefully. 'I think that your husband knows something, or his friends do, and I wanted to shake it out of him.'

Mrs Yeldon looked grim.

'I never liked the story of the street party so called.'

'You were not there.'

'Didn't like what I heard, I don't think you did.'

'You have frightened an old man. That's cruel.'

'I am cruel,' said Charmian, 'when I have to be.'

She closed the gate behind her, wondering, as she walked to her car, if she had done what was required. Looking back before she drove away, she saw that Mrs Yeldon had disappeared into the house.

She drove herself away slowly, there was a lot to think about, but as she drove, other thoughts arose: as well as being a career police officer, she was a wife whose husband needed feeding. As did the dog and cat, but she bought food for them in bulk in large packets and tins. There was no tin labelled: Husband Food, carefully prepared.

So she parked the car and sped down Peascod Street on foot to her favourite food store, picking up some tights on the way in. She was pushing her trolley down the fruit and vegetable aisle when she banged into Rewley. Literally banged in, for he was pushing his trolley one way and she was shoving hard in another.

'What are you doing here?' Silly question when his trolley was piled high with food. At

256

least he was eating, she thought.

'I have to look after myself,' he said, 'and anyway, I've got Dolly and Jim Towers coming to eat tonight. Got to do my bit, he's wearing Dolly out, there all the time. I wonder she puts up with it. Sorry for him, I suppose.'

'She likes him.'

'That too, of course.' He grinned. 'She always was one for lame dogs. But he's a decent chap. And I want to talk to him myself. See what, if anything, he has got to say about Albert ... When they got his clothes off, his back was raw, as if he had been whipping himself. That was how I smelt blood that first time.'

'That's horrible.'

'I think he did it himself. Self-flagellation, it happens. He wanted to punish himself.'

'Albert?'

'Sure. I am going to discuss it with Towers, the sort of thing he might know. He's a good man, he's really going to make something of that book, he's got the title lined up: The Morbid Kitchen. Great, isn't it? He tells me that the Institute of Criminology in London think their press might publish it. I want to talk to him about it all, see what ideas he has.'

Charmian was sceptical about the book. Was he a scholar? 'At least it takes his mind off his wife.' Then she realized what she had said. 'Sorry, clumsy of me.'

'Don't worry, I don't want to have my mind

taken off Kate. While I think about her, she is still alive. But don't play down his book, he's got some interesting ideas; he's working on the relationship between executioners and surgeons ... historically speaking, of course, And that's what I want to talk to him about, might give me some ideas on these terrible murders. Well, I must push on, I want some chicken...'

Charmian finished her own shopping, preoccupied with other things.

When she got home, she telephoned the Incident Room and asked to speak to the investigating officer. HG if he was there or the next man down. She did not know the voice on the line, but the man recognized her. 'Ask the pathologist working on Albert's body if the knife used was a surgeon's knife.'

Later that evening, after a quiet meal with her husband, she got the answer yes, it was a knife. There was a bit of extra information too: the same knife could have been used on the child's head and on Madelaine Mason. As to Margaret Drue, the work had not yet been done on her.

*   *   *

In the middle of the next day, after a peaceful night with her husband, a way of life she was beginning to appreciate (eating too much though, and certainly drinking too much wine, she had better do some serious swimming), she had a telephone call from HG himself.

'The girl has turned up.'

'Good.'

'You don't sound surprised.'

'Not sure if I am. Where was she?'

'She was found sitting in the park on a bench not far from where Albert was found. Interesting, eh?'

'What does she say?'

'Says she can remember nothing. Knows her name, and that is all.'

'What state is she in?'

'Dirty, and her clothes are torn. Bit of blood on them. No bruises that I can see but the doctor still has to examine her; his first reaction is that she had been drugged. There is a deep cut in her arm, which might be where the blood came from. Might represent a suicide attempt.'

'Or the blood might just be for decoration. For painting or writing. People have been known to use it. Primitive man, early hominids.'

HG absorbed the remark, which he did not care for, either as a joke or as a comment on the human race, saying drily: 'Well, she is not a hominid or a primitive man and whether for decoration or for suicide, she has a wound and may have others. I'll let you know.'

'I would like to see her.'

'Come round, she is in the Strait Road hospital.'

259

'What state is she in?'

There was a pause. 'Hard to say, the doctor says not bad physically . . . but she's not herself. I don't know what happened to her or what she's been through, perhaps you will make it out, but she's far away. On a cloud. I'm not sure if she really knows who she is.'

*   *   *

Emily was crouched in a chair with her head leaning on the back; her eyes were open but not seeing much; she looked shrunken. 'You won't get anything out of her,' HG had said.

Charmian touched her arm. 'Good to see you again, Emily. How are you?'

No answer.

'Do you remember me?' She answered her own question. 'I'm Charmian . . . Remember now?'

Emily just stared, then she closed her eyes without speaking.

Charmian sat looking at her for some while. A nurse came in, nodded. 'Still not talking?'; she shook her head and went out again.

Charmian leaned across and touched the girl's arm. 'Tell me, let it out, it's better you do.'

There was a pause. Then, very softly, Emily muttered: 'I can't. Don't remember.' She closed her eyes, almost as if she had not spoken.

Charmian patted the girl's wrist. 'I've had an

260

idea. I'll be back.' She looked at the girl. You took that in, she decided, your hands moved.

HG was standing in the window, looking out at the hospital car park. 'No go?'

'No, but there's something we might try. May I?' She drew him into the window and began to talk.

'OK,' he said. 'Try, but get permission from the doctor first.'

'Oh, I will do. Will you stay around?'

'No, just let me know. I'm off.'

To tell you the truth, Charmian said under her breath, it's a relief. I don't want you around watching. It might inhibit us.

And this might take some negotiating. Strangely, however, it did not. The doctor, a youngish man, gave her a long, considering look and nodded. 'Try it. She's an enigma to me . . . physically, just a bruise on the head, but miles away. If you can get her back, good luck to you.'

There was caution and scepticism of a healthy kind in his voice. Charmian thought she liked him. 'Want to watch?'

He shook his head. 'Leave it all to you. Do magic.'

Magic it is, Charmian thought an hour later as she ushered Birdie into the room where Emily still sat, black magic.

Birdie was calm, her eyes bright and alert. Round her neck swung a crystal ball which caught the light on all its many facets. She went

261

straight up to Emily and took her hand. 'Now I am going to help you back into yourself, my dear. But we must do it together. It's all there inside you and we will get out what happened to you, then you will feel better.'

She looked at Charmian and mouthed silently: We hope.

'Sit up, dear, and look at the ball which I am holding before you.'

Emily sat up with care, and Charmian, who was watching her closely, thought something stirred again at the back of her eyes. Good.

Birdie swung the crystal ball slowly, slowly in a low arc; the light caught it as it moved and it glittered with little chinks of light. 'Watch what I do, follow the lights, let them sink into your mind ... So and so and so.'

Her voice was very soft and persuasive. 'Watch what it does, follow, follow, follow.'

Emily let her eyes move as the ball moved. She was breathing deeply now, and a flush was coming up on her throat. Charmian watched with interest as the colour moved up her cheeks and on to her forehead.

'You want to help me,' Birdie intoned. 'You want to help me, you want to come back ... inside yourself, you know what happened to you, now you must tell us.'

Emily sighed. 'Blackness ... dark, I am in the dark ...'

Charmian leaned forward. 'Ask her what happened in her room. How did she hurt her arm?'

'What happened, Emily, how did you cut your arm? ... Where did the blood in the basin come from?'

Her, of course, thought Charmian.

'I cut myself,' said Emily; her eyes were closed now, she was not watching the ball or anything, but breathing deeply and regularly. 'I remember doing that ... then I was in prison, in the dark.'

'What was it like in prison?'

'Dark ... black ... it smelt.'

'What did it smell of, Emily?'

She didn't answer.

'Come on, you remember. Tell us what your prison smelt of?'

'Wood,' she said; the words were ground out of her, against her will. 'Wood,' came out again.

She opened her eyes sharply. 'Charmian?'

Birdie sat back. 'That's it. Over. We shan't get any more out of her.'

Charmian considered what she had heard. 'What did you make of that?'

'Don't ask me,' said Birdie, and she shrugged. 'Ask yourself.'

Darkness, a black prison, the smell of wood. It sounded like a coffin.

CHAPTER ELEVEN

'What did I say?' asked the girl.

'The prison ... do you remember saying you had been imprisoned?'

Emily shook her head, she frowned. 'No, I'm not sure. Perhaps I do. It's kind of cloudy.'

'And that you cut your own arm?'

Emily frowned. 'Did I say so? I may have done that,' she sounded lost. 'I shall never know.' She looked at Charmian with a question in her eyes.

'Oh, I think we will work it out,' said Charmian briskly. 'In the end.' She patted the girl's hand. 'Stay there, you'll be looked after while I sort out somewhere for you to go. You can't go back to your own place just yet.' She wondered if Emily knew about Albert or not. Probably best not to mention him just yet. Nor the discovery of Margaret Drue's remains. Leave a lot unsaid. 'What about going to stay with Dr Yeldon and his wife?'

She looked in Emily's face as she spoke. 'No? Well, we will see. Meanwhile you are here. Safe. Looked after.' And the rest of us are no doubt safer because you are here.

She went out into the hall where Birdie was standing in the window embrasure talking to the doctor. 'What did you make of that?'

Birdie shook her head. 'I don't know. Not

sure exactly what came out of my little session. I think she was under when she said about cutting herself. And just for a flash when she described where she had been. She could not hold it back.'

'I see.' She thought she did.

The doctor said: 'I have to say that I have not been convinced by the amnesia fugue, not entirely.'

'Thank you,' said Charmian. 'That's a very honest comment which I appreciate.'

'We'll keep her here overnight, but beyond that...' he shrugged. 'Hospitals never have spare rooms.'

'I will find somewhere safe for her to go,' said Charmian. She looked at Birdie.

Birdie said that she supposed they could, but she would have to consult Winifred. 'What about Dr Yeldon?'

Charmian shook her head. 'Dr Yeldon is not a happy man.'

'There's Eddy Bell ... no, I suppose not. Doesn't she have any other friends?'

'Does she need somewhere safe?' asked the doctor.

'I think she does.'

'Are you taking a high moral line?' Birdie asked.

'Something like that,' said Charmian. 'Of course, there are other people involved.' Like HG, but he would gladly devolve any responsibility for the girl on to Charmian.

265

That went without saying.

Birdie returned to talk to Winifred, the doctor to do a ward round, and Charmian went back to her own office.

On her desk were the reports from HG's team of detectives working on the associated cases: where they came in, the finding of the body of Madelaine Mason, with the head of the child Alana. A sick imagination at work here was the judgement, but no clue as yet. So long ago, would they ever find out? Speculation suggested that Mason had tried some blackmail and been killed for it.

She pushed all the reports on this case aside, worthless, a dead end: they had lined Margaret Drue up for the killer and all the time she was dead herself these many years.

Then there was Albert who had beaten his own back till it was raw because he felt guilt. The masked man, terrified, but willing to talk for money so he could escape. Albert had not escaped.

Emily had not escaped either. Or had she? Had she escaped into her own mind?

Not too many factual, scientific reports on either Margaret Drue or on Albert as yet, too early. But bound together in her mind, all these killings were moving together to make a whole picture. The mind demanded that you rationalize what you have, make it all fit together. Not the random killings of a serial murderer, not at all, reason rejected it. These deaths were connected, because all the people, alive as well as dead, knew each other.

That was how Charmian saw it: 'It's a whole thing,' she said aloud to the wall, which often heard her observations but never answered. In the old days, when Dolly Barstow had reigned alone in the outer office, she had often heard the voice of her SRADIC boss and smiled. The new pair looked surprised.

To her surprise, H. G. Horris knocked at the door, walked in to sit opposite her desk and look depressed. He had nothing to contribute but the complaint that he wasn't getting anywhere. 'I've been chewing Eddy Bell up to see what I can get from him about Albert. Damn it, the man worked for him, but nothing comes from Eddy. He says Albert wasn't a talker although a good worker but not bright. He only employed him for old times' sake.'

'Well, we know that.'

'I'm keeping quiet about finding Drue's body but I think the local press is on to it, so that silence won't last long. We shall have the whole media circus hanging round when her death comes out.'

Together they discussed all the material that was coming in from the men and women on the streets and banging on the doors to ask questions. Patient work was dredging up this and that. Such as the fact that Madelaine Mason had a nasty reputation as a watcher of young lovers, and that she had once been accused of blackmail. But nothing had come of it and the case had been dropped.

It also appeared, although it seemed to be no help to anyone, that the Bailey school might have closed anyway since it was badly in debt. Nancy was liked, the father was not, and hardly anyone remembered Emily.

'Bloody useless,' said HG.

He got up. 'Well, I only came in to be cheered up.'

'I can't believe I'm much good at it.'

'Better than you think. You are so reasonable, you see, you make me feel reason will prevail and I don't often feel like that.'

'I hope it's true.' It had never struck her before that HG had moods, he always seemed resolutely downbeat.

'Now don't you start.' He was lumbering towards the door. 'You don't know what a figure you are in this town. We point to you.'

The horrible thought came to Charmian that HG was flattering her for a purpose. But what purpose? She looked at him, wanting to ask, but not wanting the answer.

Then he provided it, but nicely and modestly, more so than she might have expected. 'My eldest granddaughter wants to join the force. Saw her this weekend and she talked about it. I didn't know what to say to her. I wondered if I might bring her to meet you? Explain to her what she's in for, the paths to follow, that sort of thing.'

'Of course.' So she was a role model? Ah, well she had been used that way before. Probably Dolly Barstow had looked at her and taken notes, so Dolly could be useful to her now. 'What's her name?'

'Phyllida.'

'How old?'

'She'll be twenty. She has a degree from Reading. Law and politics.'

'A good degree to have. Yes, I'd like to meet her. Set it up. And Inspector Barstow might come along and talk.'

'Thank you, you'll like her, I think. I do, I get on with her better than my own daughter, but that's often the way, isn't it?'

At the door, he turned. 'Oh, I forgot to say, that query of yours about the knife used on cutting the head … Yes, it could have been a surgical knife … just could have been.'

'Thank you. Confirms a notion that I had.'

He gave her a long, calm look … Was this, after all, why he had come? 'Let me know if anything comes of it.'

'Oh, I will, for sure.'

She finished her work, then returned to Maid of Honour Row for another quiet evening. Alone this time, as Humphrey was on a plane to Brussels.

She did not sleep well, she had got used to having a husband, a comfortable human figure to whom you could murmur when you could not sleep and not worry if no answer came because just the nearness was enough. Then as dawn came, she gave up the struggle to sleep and went into the sitting room where the cat at once joined her, delighted to have early morning company.

Snatches of conversation that had long rested, undigested, in her mind came back to her. She could hear Dolly Barstow's voice saying: There was a low-key story that there was something odd, unpleasant, going on in the school. She had asked: What sort of thing?

Sex, Dolly had said, hint of child abuse. A woman who sold newspapers in the town had passed on the gossip. Dead herself, now.

And then there was what Jack, Kate's father, had had to say when she had talked with him. At the time she had believed the dead body found with Alana's head had been Margaret Drue. Now she knew it was not. No matter, it did not touch what he had reported.

Margaret Drue, not a totally nice woman, as he had admitted, yet better than was said, had told him there was, exact words, 'some sex game going on among those kids'.

Little bits of information were slotting into place. The picture had always been there at the back of her mind, but now it was floating upwards like a long buried relic.

I am not sure if I know where to start, she told herself, aware that her head was aching.

She went to her office, looked over the day's engagements, cancelled two, and drove to the

270

hospital.

It was still early, ten thirty in the morning, with the sun out in a blue sky, but cold. She felt cold.

The hospital entrance hall was crowded with patients making towards the right clinic, looking for the ward where they were expected, with other people, visitors presumably, shopping for flowers and newspapers in the hospital shop. There was a coffee shop close by in the hospital arcade which was already crowded.

Charmian, for a moment at a loss, with her head still aching, made her way to the second-floor ward where Emily had been tucked away in a small side-room all to herself. She tapped on the door, and went in. The room was empty. It was quieter up here, but even so it was hard to capture the attention of anyone. At the end of the corridor, a nurse in a smart blue uniform spared her a minute.

'Miss Bailey discharged herself, and left early this morning ... She was free to do that.'

'Yes, of course.' Damn the girl. 'Did she say where she was going?'

The nurse shook her head. 'She may have told Sister.'

Sister, interrupted in her morning rounds, knew nothing. 'No, I'm sorry. She didn't say. She wasn't really ill, you know, we would have been discharging her today in any case.' As Charmian turned away, the Sister added

271

thoughtfully: 'I have an idea she left with someone ... a woman.'

Her head still aching, Charmian went back to the shop on the ground floor, bought some aspirin, then took herself next door for a cup of coffee which, to her surprise and pleasure, was hot and strong. Then she went back to her car to telephone. First Birdie and Winifred.

'Is Emily with you?'

'No, certainly not.' It was Winifred who answered. 'Birdie told me you suggested we have her here. The answer is yes, we will, of course, but she is not here now.'

One more call, this time to Dr Yeldon. 'Doctor, I know this is a long shot, but is Emily Bailey with you?'

He sounded flustered, but clear all the same. Emily was not with him, he was home alone, and had not seen the girl for weeks. Perhaps longer.

She made one more call. 'Dolly, glad I found you in.'

'Just going out, off to London on the Vander case, your idea, remember.' Dolly had not fancied the Vander case for herself, another boring fraud. 'What can I do?'

'You've almost answered what I wanted to know already ... Emily Bailey is not with you?'

'No.' Dolly did not sound surprised, she had learnt never to show surprise. 'Haven't seen the girl. You want her? Can't help.'

'Dolly, I am going down to see Eddy Bell in

272

his workshop. Forget London and come down and join me there. You know the way?'

'Think so.'

Charmian drove into the town, parked her car by the river, walked over Eton Bridge, which only allows foot passengers, turned left at the bottom and walked about a hundred yards along the river bank. There was a small, ancient grey church to pass, and a graveyard where a funeral had recently taken place, she could see wreaths on a new grave. One wreath missing, she thought.

And next door was the place she was looking for: Eddy Bell's. Bell's Yard, it said on a large board, where his father and his grandfather before him had had their workplace. It was quiet and rather shabby but not unprosperous, the Bells were known to be good workmen, each in their day, even Eddy now. But the new road, long planned and now to be built, would run through here, and force the Bells to move from the present site. Things would not go on here as they had done for so long.

But there was no one in the outer yard, so she walked through the archway at the back, past piled up timber and ladders all in orderly disorder. Eddy's lorry was parked here, as well as a small van.

A doorway led into a barn, high and gloomy, not much light got in; there were more planks, more scaffolding, all smelling of dust and paint. The wood, some of which looked

273

ancient, as if it had been bought by an early Bell to build a house for a Victorian artisan, seemed to be piled up to create alcoves of darkness.

She heard a girl laugh. Not a happy laugh but one with pain in it. Why did you come back here, Emily, to this place next door to a graveyard? But she could answer that herself: where else to go when you are at the end of everything, but into hell. This would do for hell.

A light, unsteady laugh with a note of fear in it.

Charmian moved forward slowly into the dusk. 'Emily? Is that you? Are you there?'

Then she could see Emily sitting on a piece of sacking in one of the alcoves. No wonder so much dust of wood and stone had got into and on to all the bodies.

'Emily!'

Eddy Bell appeared through a gap behind the girl. 'Miss Daniels.' He was polite, not welcoming but not going to be rude. If he could help it.

Charmian stood still: the darkness, the dusty smell of wood, the closeness of it all, came home to her. Here was Emily's 'prison'. This was where she had been, whether imprisoned or not. No matter what other lies, what ignorance she might have pretended to, the truth had popped out about this. Birdie had achieved that much.

She took a step forward. 'So this is where you have been.'

Eddy came forward. 'What's all this about, Miss Daniels? You've got me there ... What is it with Em? I call her Em, don't I, Em?'

Emily nodded.

'She won't say much, she's a bit speechless at the moment. She cut herself, did you know that? Silly girl, she was doing it when I went to call on her, so I brought her back here. To tell you the truth, I think you lot have frightened her. Put the wind up her.'

'I think she's been frightened a long time.' And had wanted to come out into the open. Why else had she let Charmian into the basement? 'Did you send that silly wreath? I can see where you might have got it from.'

Eddy didn't answer, just gave a laugh. 'It's always a pity to waste a good set of flowers ... Come through to my office, it's round the back.'

Still talking cheerfully, he led the way to a small room lit by a single central electric light. Against one wall was a huge old desk, with an ancient typewriter. The telephone, however, was modern, and there was a fax machine. A big chest-refrigerator and freezer sat on another wall.

'My old dad's office and his dad before him. I've left it much as it was, haven't bothered, but I have added one or two touches of my own.' He folded away the local newspaper he had been reading, but Charmian noticed it.

He saw her looking. 'I always take it, we advertise in it ourselves...'

No need to ask where Madelaine Mason had found her piece of newspaper.

An overall, none too clean, hung on the door, and an open shelf was lined with drills, hammers and odd bits of oily builder's tools. Charmian let her eyes run over them. An oil can, draped with old rags, stood underneath. The rag, like the refrigerator, interested her.

'Do sit down, please.' Eddy seemed to have put himself in charge, which Charmian did not care for.

'I want you, Emily, and you too, Eddy, to come down to Superintendent Horris's office to answer some questions.'

'Whatever for? Em, what you have you been doing? What have you been up to?'

Emily stood where she was without answering.

'She's not talking too well at the moment, Miss Daniels, I don't know what's come over her.'

'She can talk well enough when she has to,' said Charmian. 'Or when she is made to.' She directed her words to the girl. 'A prison, you said, Emily, dark and dusty ... this is it, isn't it? I am not sure if you wanted those words to pop out, but they did. It is very hard to keep silent in this world, words have a way of pushing to the top. It's called guilt, I think.' She added:

276

'Albert saw guilt in someone's face, saw a real horror peeping out of the eyes.'

Eddy started to talk but Emily spoke then, her voice suddenly sharp and hard. 'Shut up, Eddy, stop making a fool of yourself.'

'She's right. But I will speak and you will listen. When I first picked up the talk about the sex play in the school, I didn't know what to make of it. It didn't sound like anything I had heard about that school that Nancy Bailey ran so successfully. She may not have been wise in one or two of her staff, maybe she did have a blind streak that misled her, so that she employed a woman like Margaret Drue and another like Madelaine Mason, but she tried to be careful and good with her school. I didn't believe she would let anything touch her pupils. On every level, they were valuable to her.'

'Please,' said Emily. 'Don't go on. I've had enough of this already.'

'But then I remembered that there was another group of schoolchildren associated with that household but overlooked. Not pupils there, but at another school, but who knew their way about the Bailey premises. Who probably absented themselves from their own school without anyone caring much. You, of course, Eddy and Emily and Albert.'

Eddy said: 'I'll kill you.'

'Thank you, Eddy, and I am sure you would like to. Emily's frightened of you, that's why

277

she got away. What did you do to her down here, Eddy? She had already tried to slash her wrists ... Or did you do that for her?'

'Anything on Em is self-inflicted,' said Eddy. 'I don't say anything about anything else. And I didn't fetch her back here. Ask another.'

'You were three strong youngsters, playing sex games. Helped by drugs, Eddy? There's a funny smell down here that reminds me of it. Still on it, are you? That would account for something. I'll ask you later where you get the stuff, but I can guess who started you off.' She put out her hand. 'No, stay where you are. I'm talking now ... The child Alana must have seen you three, playing some sex tricks together. The Bailey garden has some secluded corners and outbuildings. So you killed her, all of you or one of you. Were you high on something, Eddy?'

A sound escaped Emily, it might have been a no.

'About the head cutting off, well, we will go into that later ... But I suppose Madelaine Mason saw something that made her wonder, saw you, or guessed it was you and perhaps came to you later, she was something of a blackmailer so I have heard. She too was killed. Did you keep her body here? Plenty of places, that's my guess, and when the school closed and Nancy moved away and the house was empty for so long, you, Eddy, builder Eddy Bell, were well placed to tuck the body away

278

here. She couldn't stay with you, nor the head in the fridge, because the new road is coming through here and you knew it. So you moved the head and the body to where it looked safer. Did someone advise you to do that, Eddy?

'It must have been a bad moment when you realized that the place had to be opened up. As it would not have been if the place was left outright to Emily.

'Madelaine Mason was killed because she saw or guessed something and was set for a bit of blackmail, but Margaret Drue had already gone, hadn't she? Killed because she knew it was you three.'

'Rubbish talk.'

'No, guessing, but not rubbish, and there will be traces in your van and your refrigerator even after all this time. You killed Margaret Drue and you and Albert buried her. I am not saying it was all your idea ... you took advice from someone older.'

Two deaths and two more to come, Charmian thought; she was talking hard in the hope that Dolly would appear soon.

'Albert lost his nerve, didn't he? He was going to tell all and then run away, because he suddenly saw madness, evil, in the eyes of a person he had known a long time. It popped out, he said. He wasn't bright but he saw that, and because of it he was killed. Was it you, Eddy? I have some thoughts there. Guilty and strong you are, Eddy, but are you strong

279

enough for all that evil?'

Eddy was standing close to her, she could smell his breath. He had been drinking and perhaps had smoked a loaded cigarette.

'But don't try and play innocent, Eddy, because you are both guilty and stupid. I'll tell you why you are stupid. Over there, you have a can with oil in, and as an oil rag you are using a bit of striped cotton. I can't see the colour very well, because it is so dirty, but I saw the stripe, and the scientists are so skillful they will bring out the colour and say yes, the colour and the fibres match the skirt on Madelaine Mason.'

Yellow stripes for Madelaine Mason, orange for Margaret Drue, this had looked yellow. She was imprisoned here, poor yellow-skirted soul, and wrote to me on a bit of your newspaper.

Eddy moved away from her, to look behind her as if there was a noise.

'I seemed to sense another figure behind you, a fourth person, older and wicked. I thought it must be Margaret Drue at first but I maligned her ... no, it turns out she was dead all the time.'

She could hear movement behind her.

'So who is this other person in the shadows, there all the time, using you, corrupting you?'

She half turned. 'Is that you, Dolly?'

It was then she felt the hands coming from behind her, and the knife at her throat.

There are times to be brave, and times where

280

it has no point, times to scream for help and times when you cannot. Charmian did not feel brave and with a knife at her throat she could not scream. As it was, she could feel the sharp edge scratching her skin.

'Don't try to kill me, plenty of people know that I came down here. And one of my officers is on the way now.'

I hope she arrives before you cut my head off, she thought. 'And I know who *you* are,' she said as loudly she could. 'I heard your laugh on the tape.'

'Heads are safer off,' said an answering voice. 'You know they are dead for sure.'

The Queen was right, thought Charmian, there is a practical reason for cutting off the head. A bead of blood rolled down her neck. By God, if I am going to die, I am going to take this lot with me. Somehow.

But it was Emily who moved. She screamed, and then perhaps realizing that it would be her throat next, she fainted. She fell against Charmian and her attacker, knocking them all three to the ground.

Charmian felt the knife bite into her neck as they fell. She could sense it tear into the flesh. My throat is cut, she said to herself, but I am going to live. I have to: there's Kate's baby, there's SRADIC, too. And I've got to beat Horris ... and there's that sizzling rumour just going round about his young girlfriend ...

281

must stay alive to hear the end of that. Can you laugh as you die?

Behind her, she could hear Dolly shouting: 'Held up by that bloody security alert.' And there was a man's voice too. Was it Rewley?

As darkness clouded her eyes, she knew, no, not Rewley, she recognized the tones: it was Jim Towers. She had just the vital spirit left to grasp she would be part of his book.

Extract from *The Place of the Head* or *The Morbid Kitchen* by James Towers

An extract from Chapter V: Heads Lost. The Case of Mrs Mary Yeldon

...this interesting case in a Berkshire town nearly resulted in the decapitation of a high-ranking police officer. All the officers who worked on the case, Chief Superintendent Daniels, Superintendent Horris and Inspector George Rewley, found it a difficult and painful investigation.

A series of murders took place for which three people, Eddy Bell, Emily Bailey and the prime instigator of the whole ill doings, an older person, wife of a revered local doctor, Mrs Mary Yeldon, stood trial. All three were found guilty of the murders; Bell and Bailey are serving prison sentences and Yeldon is in a mental hospital. The trial illustrates the importance of the Dead Head.

To Mrs Yeldon, whose sexual activities of

voyeur and child abuser led her to murder, the head had great importance. She regarded the victim's head as the source of all vital power, and there is some evidence she continued to talk to the child's head. She is now in a high-security mental institution. The sexual games in which she encouraged the youngsters to indulge did not involve the innocent pupils of a school owned by the Bailey family, but they brought about the death of one child and the subsequent deaths of two teachers at the school. In addition they ruined the lives of several people concerned and broke up the family of Dr Yeldon.

The case has a special interest because there is evidence that the head was first frozen for some years (the body of another victim being stored in some place where there was wood dust) and then both head and body were moved when a road development threatened the site. In this second hiding place, in an old kitchen, the head was boiled.

The police officer, Chief Superintendent Charmian Daniels, recovered.

Note: Much interesting evidence was given by Miss Clara Meldrum, a graduate and former pupil at Miss Bailey's School, who was the girlfriend of one of the killers. She said Eddy

Bell was a nice chap and she had no idea what he was really like. She never got to know Emily Bailey well, but Mrs Yeldon was a terror, and the children had called her the 'Dragon'.

We hope you have enjoyed this Large Print book. Other Chivers Press or Thorndike Press Large Print books are available at your library or directly from the publishers.

For more information about current and forthcoming titles, please call or write, without obligation, to:

Chivers Press Limited
Windsor Bridge Road
Bath BA2 3AX
England
Tel. (01225) 335336

OR

Thorndike Press
P.O. Box 159
Thorndike, Maine 04986
USA
Tel. (800) 223–2336

All our Large Print titles are designed for easy reading, and all our books are made to last.